A DAY TO GO HUNTING

Christine Pullein-Thompson lives in a moated Rectory in Suffolk. She is married to author Julian Popescu, and they have four children. She wrote her first book while still in her teens, and has had more than sixty books published since then.

She began riding when she was six, and had fallen off more than a hundred times before she was twelve. At one time, she ran the Grove Riding School with her sisters, Josephine and twin Diana, when they had more than forty horses in their stables. She also whipped-in to the Woodland Foxhounds, competed across country, show jumped, and was a South Berkshire Gymkhana Champion. She still rides and has three horses, a dog and a cat.

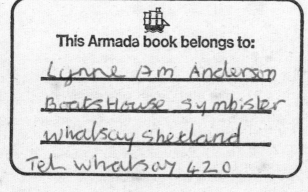

This Armada book belongs to:

Lynne Am Anderson

BoatsHouse symbister

whalsay shetland

Tel whalsay 420

Other titles by Christine Pullein-Thompson in Armada

Phantom Horse
Phantom Horse Comes Home
Phantom Horse Goes to Ireland
Phantom Horse in Danger
Phantom Horse Goes to Scotland
Stolen Ponies
The Horse Sale
I Rode a Winner
Ride By Night

Good Riding
Riding for Fun
Improve Your Riding

First published in the U.K. in 1956 by William Collins
Sons & Co. Ltd., London and Glasgow. This edition was
first published in Armada in 1969 by
Fontana Paperbacks,
14 St. James's Place, London SW1A 1PS.

This impression 1981

© Christine Pullein-Thompson 1956

Printed in Great Britain by
Love & Malcomson Ltd.,
Brighton Road, Redhill, Surrey.

A DAY TO GO
HUNTING

CHRISTINE PULLEIN-THOMPSON

Armada

List of Main Characters

ANGELA: 12, has dark hair, is an only child, owns *Moonlight*

JOHN: 16, is the son of a farmer, the only horsy member of a large family, owns *Quickstep*

MR AND MRS PIERCE: proprietors of The Riding School

JANE: 16, is their girl groom: she hunts *Trooper*

ADAM: 12, is small and wears spectacles. Son of the Vicar, he rides *Sandy* from The Riding School

TONY: 16, is the daughter of well-off parents, hunts *Southwind* and has a show-jumper called *Roderick*

THE TRUMANS: Professor and Mrs Truman hunt *Cloudy* and *Copper*. They have three daughters—

JEAN: 12, dark haired. Hunts *Black Knight*

ANNE: 10, with chestnut hair

HARRIET: 9, red haired. Hunts *Melody*

GRAHAM: 13, has ginger hair. Rides *Jumbo* from The Riding School

MARK: 11, is the cobbler's son, has red hair and freckles, owns *Merrylegs*

LUCY: 10, has fair curly hair, rides *Midnight* from The Riding School

MR JEEVES: Master

THE HUNT STAFF

BILL SMART: Huntsman

BRUCE: First Whipper-in

CAPTAIN FREEMANTLE: Amateur Second Whipper-in

SAM: Head Groom and Second Horseman

TOM: Stable Lad

CHAPTER ONE

ANGELA WALKED across the orchard calling, "Moonie, Moonie, Moonlight," a small, dumpy figure with large blue eyes and dark hair cut in a fringe. After a time the grey pony stopped stripping bark off an orange pippin tree and came towards her.

It had been raining and the grass was still wet. Looking at the grey sky, Angela thought, perhaps there'll be a scent, perhaps we'll have the run of the season. Hounds were to meet at Betchley on the following day and, though Angela was no horsewoman and Moonlight old and slow, they were both mad about hunting. Angela would cheerfully hack fourteen miles to a meet and return in pitch darkness to the small white-washed cottage where she lived.

Now Moonlight obligingly pushed his broad grey nose into the halter Angela carried. He was clipped trace high and came in at night to the little loose-box next to the garage. Angela talked to him as she led him back across the orchard.

"You're filthy. You'll certainly have to have your tail washed. Why did you have to go and roll? You were quite clean this morning," she said.

Wistaria and jasmine climbed the cottage walls. Angela's bedroom looked towards the tall beech woods which were scattered haphazard across the Flintshire hills.

She led Moonlight into the loose-box where she had put hay and a feed ready for him and went indoors to fetch a bucket of soapy water for his tail.

Her mother was toasting crumpets. "Don't be too long, darling," she said, "it's nearly tea time."

Angela said, "Okay, Mummy. But I must wash his tail. It's filthy."

"I love you even if you are slow and can't jump more than two foot six," Angela told Moonlight as she worked. "And I'm rotten at riding anyway, so even if you were the most brilliant pony in the world, we still wouldn't win any prizes."

Angela was twelve, and though she had been riding for six years she had never won more than a third prize in an obstacle race. She was a girl guide, and preferred the poorer children of the village to the ones who rode at the local riding school, who were inclined to laugh at Moonlight and think her feeble; she spent most of her week-ends giving lessons on Moonlight to children who had no pony of their own. Her father was in advertising and the Clavers were by way of being what the local people called "arty."

Angela knew that she was growing out of Moonlight. Several people had dropped hints to that effect lately, including Mr. and Mrs. Pierce, who ran the riding school, and Jane, the girl who worked for them. Angela didn't know what she would do when she really couldn't ride Moonlight any more. Except for a Shetland she had owned in her extreme youth, she had always ridden him, until now she was scared to ride anything else.

Let's see, Betchley's five miles away so we had better leave around nine-thirty, Angela thought, rinsing Moonlight's tail. I hope Mummy's washed my gloves for me. And I *do* hope hounds don't run like mad across the vale or I shall be left behind in the first five minutes.

*   *   *

Four miles the other side of Betchley, John Simons laid down his tools. The son of a farmer, he had been mixing concrete for the new piggeries. Now his back ached and his hands felt like sandpaper. I suppose I'd better clean my tack, he thought, seeing it in his mind's eye hanging stiff and dirty on the brackets in the old farm stable.

He was the only horsy member of a large family; George, his elder brother, was studying to become a chemist. His two sisters, Julie and Sally, were more interested in film stars and fashions, and his younger brother, Peter, was terrified of all animals, but most of all, cows.

As he crossed the yard, Quickstep, his chestnut hunter, whinnied to him. She was a lightweight mare of fifteen two, with a star and two white socks, and she was the apple of John's eye.

"I won't be a sec'," he told her, "I must put these things away first."

He thought, I hope Tony's out to-morrow. Tony's real name was Antonia Selwyn Jones. She lived in the old Manor house which her parents had done up. Her father was in business and extremely well off, so that he was able to buy Tony expensive show ponies and a fourteen two hunter called Southwind, and employ a groom. Locally Tony was supposed to be conceited and a bit of a pot hunter, but to John she was a constant source of admiration. In optimistic moments he imagined her coming to tea in the grey stone farmhouse where he lived. But so far he hadn't managed to invite her.

Now he mixed Quickstep a feed of oats, bran, chaff and cow cake. Then he filled a bucket with water and started to clean his tack.

* * *

The yard of Mr. and Mrs. Pierce's riding school was full of pupils. Janet and Susan Chandler were fighting in a corner over a dandy brush. Adam was looking for a hoof-pick. Mr. Pierce was showing a client a big bay hunter called Bombshell. Mrs. Pierce was hogging a black pony's mane, and fair-haired, sixteen-year-old Jane was cleaning tack assisted by Margery, Lucy, Joan, Graham and David.

7

Jane had been working for the Pierces for the last six months. To-morrow she was to hunt a young thoroughbred called Trooper, and she wasn't at all happy about it. To begin with he was only four, and he had received very little schooling. His few jumping lessons had been in the lane and she had only ridden him once before. She had been told to ride him in a twisted snaffle and running martingale and, though she didn't set up to be an expert, she was certain an egg-butt snaffle and drop noseband would have been a better choice.

Jane had no parents. They had both been killed in a car crash. She had lived with different aunts until becoming the Pierces' girl groom. Now, while she cleaned tack, she thought, but it isn't worth quarrelling with one's bread and butter. I must try and stay here for a year, then perhaps I shall be able to get a better job. In her youth she had been taught riding by a continental expert and her views on equitation differed widely from the Pierces'. In her opinion Trooper was not yet ready to hunt.

At last Adam found the hoof pick tangled up with the hay string in the Dutch barn. Small, wiry, with spectacles, he possessed tireless energy. He was completely reckless and rode without thought for his own or his horse's safety. In the hunting field he was known as a thruster and was inclined to gallop over crops because he didn't see them. With wildly flapping arms and legs, he would win bending, potato and obstacle races with surprising frequency. And once he had won the Children's Jumping at a nearby show, through sheer determination.

Now he hurried to Sandy's loose-box and flung open the door wide enough for the dun pony to dodge past him and gallop gaily across the yard.

Jane said, "Oh Adam!" and left the tack. The black pony jumped sideways on to Mrs. Pierce's toe and Janet and Susan Chandler stopped fighting.

Adam cried, "It wasn't my fault. He dodged past me."

Jane said, "Whoa, Sandy. Good boy."

"You should have caught him by the mane," Lucy told Adam.

It was twenty minutes before Jane managed to catch Sandy and by that time she was feeling quite cross. She put him back in his box and said, "For goodness' sake don't do it again," to Adam; and returned to cleaning tack.

Susan and Janet, who lived in the village and were going to follow hounds in their mother's car, started to fill up the horses' water buckets. Adam picked out Sandy's hoofs, which wasn't necessary because Jane had done it in the morning, and then started to groom him. Mr. Pierce took his client into the house and watched him write a cheque for two hundred and fifty pounds.

* * *

In the Manor House Tony was combing Brutus, her Boxer puppy. She was sixteen, exactly six months younger than John. Like Angela she was an only child. She had short dark curly hair, brown eyes and a nose which turned up at the end. In spite of what people said, she was not conceited. When she didn't answer it was not because she was too superior to notice other people, but because her mind was miles away, hunting, jumping Roderick in a show, or thinking about a book she had just read. She didn't even consider herself a very good rider. She thought she won prizes because her father bought her expensive ponies and she had been well taught. Sometimes she even wished that her parents were poor, so that she could look after her ponies herself like other children.

"You'll be able to go for a walk with Mummy and Daddy to-morrow," she told Brutus now. She thought, I hope Mundy gives Southwind enough oats, and saw herself galloping across the quiet, tawny December fields, the wind in her face and the cry of hounds in her ears.

* * *

Half-way between Betchley and Angela's home Professor Truman and his family were having tea. To-morrow they would all be hunting except for Anne, whose turn had come to stay at home and make the bran mashes for the others' return. Ursula, a stocky German girl, who helped Mrs. Truman look after the family, would be there to keep her company. Anne was ten and a half, with chestnut hair and blue eyes. Harriet, nine, with wild red hair, would be riding brown, twelve two Melody; Jean, who was dark, with grey eyes like her mother, would be mounted on Black Knight, a sturdy Fell pony. Professor and Mrs. Truman would be riding dapple-grey Cloudy, and liver chestnut Copper.

"I hope there's a south-west wind to-morrow," Harriet said now, stuffing currant loaf and butter into her mouth. "Do you think there will be, Mummy?"

"Most likely," her mother answered. "It's in the west now, but of course anything might happen in the night."

They had all spent the afternoon grooming the horses. They lived in a stone house which had once been a mill. In earlier times the stables which housed their hunters had been used for work horses who had carted away the flour ground by the mill. In the summer the whole Truman family would often be seen shrieking, splashing one another and swimming in the river below their house.

* * *

A quarter of a mile from Betchley, red-headed Mark Little was brushing Merrylegs. His father was a cobbler and Mark kept his roan Welsh pony in the little paddock behind the shop. In his spare time Mark collected and delivered shoes, which was supposed to pay for his pony's keep. He was small for his eleven years, with freckles and a snub nose. An ardent member of the Pony Club, he was known to be sporting and was always the first there when there was a gate to be opened in the hunting field.

Mark had three sisters who occasionally rode Merrylegs, but they weren't keen and never wanted to ride in gymkhanas, nor to hunt. Mark and Merrylegs frequently won the musical chairs at the local shows and were immensely popular with the crowd.

Now he finished grooming Merrylegs and untied her from the paddock fence. "And don't you go and roll," he said, watching her trot away.

He went into the new council house where he lived and smelt fish cooking for tea.

*   *   *

Bill Smart, huntsman to the South Flintshire Foxhounds, was standing in the kennel yard with his whipper-in, Bruce. Together they looked at hounds and decided which ones they would take on the following day.

This was Bill Smart's first season with the Flintshire and so far he had been dogged with misfortune, until he was beginning to wonder whether he would be given notice in February. First there had been a dry spell and scent had been non-existent. Then it had rained day after day, washing away all trace of any foxes. And now it was December and so far they hadn't had one decent day's hunting.

"I'll take old Thunder. He may be too old like the Master says, but he's reliable, which is more than some of these young ones are," he said now, looking at a heavy-jowled, long-backed dog hound.

Bill's surname suited him; he had sharp features, a determined chin, and eyes like a hawk. When hunting, he carried what he called a compass in his head and was never lost however far from home he might be.

Bruce was tall and lanky. His eyes were blue and he

11

had the soft accent of Somerset where he had been born and bred.

"I suppose you'll be taking Raiment and Rueful," he said, pointing to a couple of light-coloured hounds.

"Yes. If we leave old Warrior, the three bitches in the other court and Whynot and Wisdom, that leaves us with fifteen and a half couple, doesn't it?" the huntsman said. "That should be enough for the vale."

"And let's hope young Captain Freemantle is in time to-morrow," Bruce said. "I bet he holds us up again."

Captain Freemantle was amateur second whipper-in to the Flintshire. A London business man of thirty-two, he was far from popular with the hunt staff. He was frequently late in arriving on hunting mornings and was generally on a pub crawl when most needed in the hunting field. However he was a friend of Mr. Jeeves, the Master, and this was his third season, so as Bill said, it seemed that he was there to stay.

"That's that then," Bill said now, thinking of tea.

"Five-thirty to-morrow morning and we leave here at nine sharp."

* * *

Captain Freemantle was in a first-class compartment of the London-Worthington express, talking to a business acquaintance.

"Should be a good scent to-morrow. I'm hunting, you know. Just a little pack, you know, but sporting. The Flintshire. Expect you've heard of them. I whip-in to them, you know."

He was smoking with a long cigarette holder, had dark hair and wore a Homburg hat.

* * *

Mr. Jeeves had just returned from the auction of a

nearby farm. He had a lean look about him, and dark hair. He had ridden regularly under National Hunt Rules until breaking his back for a second time when his wife had forced him to give it up. Now he contented himself with farming his nine-hundred-acre farm and with the Mastership of the Flintshire. He lived three miles from the kennels in a fine old Georgian house.

"I hope the laundry have sent back my hunting-ties," he said now to his wife. "Last week they lost them, you may remember."

In his mind's eye he was already galloping across the Vale on Grey Dawn, the favourite of all his hunters. He saw his beloved hounds streaming across the open fields, felt a breeze in his face, the horn between the buttons of his coat, the well-soaped reins between his fingers.

"I hope Bill shows some sport to-morrow. We've had a rotten season so far," he said. "Freemantle thinks he ought to have his notice in February."

*   *   *

In Betchley's cobbled market-place two women with shopping-baskets stood talking. "Going to the meet to-morrow?" one asked.

"Yes, I'll be there. I never miss the 'ounds," the other one replied. They walked on together through the sleepy grey town, while the wind veered to the east and the sky cleared

CHAPTER TWO

THERE WAS a frost that night, but with the dawn came rain. Angela, slipping out of her divan bed, hearing patter patter against the lattice window, thought, it *would* be wet.

Eileen, one of her week-end pupils, had insisted on coming to help get Moonlight ready. Now they met in the yard. Angela switched on the light outside the garage. And Eileen said, "I'm not late, am I? Mum forgot to call me."

Together they groomed Moonlight and washed the parts of him which were dirty. Later they plaited his long straggly mane, each starting a different end.

Mrs. Clavers cooked them bacon and eggs for breakfast, which they ate in the kitchen with its dresser hung with blue and white china and the Aga warming their cold hands and feet.

"Now do be careful, Angela darling," her mother said. "Remember the ground will be slippery after the rain."

"I'm sure to lose them in the first five minutes. I always do when we meet at Betchley. Don't be surprised if I'm back for lunch," Angela said gaily.

"I've made you some sandwiches just in case you aren't" Mrs. Clavers said.

Angela changed into jodhpurs, a yellow polo-collared sweater and a checked riding-jacket. She collected the hunting-whip, which her father had given her for her birthday, from its place in the hall, kissed her parents, thanked Eileen, mounted Moonlight and rode out into the raw December morning. Half-way to the meet she realised that she had forgotten her gloves.

*   *   *

John had been up since five helping his father milk the cows, because Bert, the old cowman who had worked for Mr. Simons for thirty-five years, was ill. Now he switched off the electric milking machine and hurried to the stable. There wasn't time to give Quickstep more than a lick and a polish, and as John worked, he thought, Bert would fall sick this morning of all mornings, and saw Southwind beautifully turned out by Mundy, and Tony immaculate in her hunting-clothes.

Struggling into his battered hunting-boots, donning his crash cap, which he could wear because his father was a farmer, he thought, the ground will be like a skating-rink. I shall have to go carefully. I don't want to crack up Quickstep. He was a quiet competent rider and rode more by instinct than anything else. He would look before he leapt and ride back to shut a gate someone else had left open.

He clattered down the old farm stairs, his blunt spurs jingling. His mother gave him a package of cheese sandwiches. She was a large woman in an overall, with her grey hair tied back with a piece of ribbon.

He looked at the weathercock over the stable as he mounted. The wind was veering all ways. The sky was clearing. His sisters waved to him as he rode out of the farmyard. "Have a good day," they shouted.

*   *   *

There was havoc at the riding school. In spite of a shoe inspection two days ago, Midnight had lost a shoe during the night. Jane had wakened at a quarter to six, when her alarm clock went off, with a headache. Sandy had again escaped from his box: while plaiting Trooper's mane she had lost her one and only needle, and Adam had upset the paraffin used in the saddle room stove. Mr. and Mrs. Pierce had overslept. Arriving in the yard at seven-thirty they had blamed Jane for everything. Now riding Midnight bareback to the blacksmith's she was filled with an overwhelming sense of injustice. I shall answer an advertisement in *Horse and Hound*, she thought rebelliously, and imagined herself securing a marvellous job and riding in One Day Events. The blacksmith didn't take long to put on a new shoe. When she returned to the riding school all was still bustle and noise. Adam had put the wrong bridle on Sandy, Lucy was madly oiling hoofs. Mrs. Pierce was saddling her heavyweight grey hunter, and she called, "Hurry up, Jane. We're already half an hour behind time."

Jane felt too furious to speak. She put a forward cut saddle, a twisted snaffle and a running martingale on Trooper, gave Adam a different bridle to put on Sandy and rushed indoors to change.

Twenty minutes later she was hacking a jogging, head-tossing Trooper along a wet road with Mrs. Pierce on her grey, Adam on Sandy, Lucy on Midnight and Graham on piebald Jumbo. She still had a headache and the raw morning did nothing to disperse her ill humour. Normally she loved hunting and looked forward to a day with the Flintshire for weeks in advance. But on this occasion she felt out of sympathy with everyone—Trooper, Mrs. Pierce, the pupils. Then she remembered her sandwiches still lying on the kitchen table. I'm just hopeless to-day, she thought furiously, and then, oh *do* stop jogging, Trooper.

*   *   *

Tony came down for breakfast dressed for hunting, except for the scarf round her neck which would shortly be replaced by a white hunting tie. She was first in the dining-room and, helping herself to haddock from the electro-plated dish on the sideboard, she thought it looked a miserable day. There won't be much scent, she decided, but you never know, we might find a fox in the gorse bushes on Withy Hill.

Presently her parents came down and they discussed the chances of a good run across the vale.

Three-quarters of an hour later, Tony thanked Mundy, mounted an impatient Southwind and turned into the road.

*　　*　　*

The Trumans were all ready far too early. Mrs. Truman tied her husband's tie, tucked Harriet's red hair further under her crash cap and said, "Don't do anything silly, Anne," and "You'll look after her, won't you?" to Ursula.

Anne looked away and felt tears smarting in her eyes. She hated it when it was her turn to stay at home, and though the weather was awful she felt sure that to-day the rest of the family would enjoy the run of the season just because it wasn't her turn to go.

Jean was thinking, poor Anne, but what about me? I can't hunt at all in the term. Jean had just finished her first term at Littlewick School for girls. The Trumans were not good at turning out their horses. However hard they worked Black Knight always looked dusty, their plaits sewn with so much anguish lumpy, and Cloudy decidedly dingy.

Now they all stood talking in the kitchen, wishing time would pass more quickly so that they could start.

"I wonder who will be out to-day," Harriet said.

"The usual crowd I expect: head in the air Antonia Selwyn Jones, John Simons, the boy on the little roan pony, the riding school string," Jean answered.

The Flintshire was a small pack and you were inclined to see the same few people out week after week.

"Well, I hope Adam won't get cursed by the Master this time," said Anne, who had a kind heart.

"I'm sure we'd better start," Mrs. Truman said.

"But it's still awfully early," grumbled Jean, following the rest of the family through the back door, down to the stables, mounting Black Knight, thinking, it's wonderful to be hunting again after a whole term at school.

Without telling anyone Harriet had given Melody a double ration of oats and, as she adjusted her stirrups, she was hoping they would have the right effect.

Anne said, "Have a lovely day," and hoped she sounded cheerful. Mrs. Truman kissed her. "Don't do anything silly," she said.

Standing in the yard, hearing the river rushing beneath the mill, Anne thought, what shall I do? It'll be hours before they come back. She watched them ride away, and the rain stopped and she thought, I suppose I'd better help Ursula. Next week it'll be my turn. Harriet will be standing here then trying not to cry. Slowly, she walked indoors.

*　　*　　*

Mrs. Little called Mark. She was a rosy-cheeked woman with worn hands and endless patience.

"It's morning, Mark," she said. "Hurry up now or you won't be at Betchley by eleven."

"Thanks, Mum," Mark said, waking, sitting up, thinking, it's raining.

He dressed quickly in jodhpurs, shoes and a thick jersey. When he reached the kitchen his mother pressed a cup of steaming tea into his hand. On the table was a plate of fried potatoes and an egg.

Mark gobbled his breakfast, though it was only seven o'clock and he had plenty of time. He fetched Merrylegs's halter from the wash-house, snatched a crust of bread from the table and hurried along the road to the paddock. It was beginning to get light. Mark stood at the gate calling, "Merrylegs, Merrylegs, come on, Merrylegs." He wished now that he had put on a mackintosh; already he was wet, and where, oh where was Merrylegs? Usually he would come trotting across to him when he called. With a funny feeling in the pit of his stomach, Mark climbed the gate and started to cross the paddock still calling, "Merrylegs, Merrylegs, come on, Merrylegs." Though it was still too dark for him to see the gap in the hedge, he guessed after a time that she had gone. He stood in the middle of the paddock thinking, what shall I do? She may be miles away by now. He decided to fetch his bike and ran back across the paddock, with a lump in his throat. All the week he had been looking forward to this day, not just to the hunt, but to everything— grooming Merrylegs, watching her eat her feed, riding to the meet, talking to other members of the Pony Club, hunting, hacking home in the dusk, telling the family all about his day. Now as he climbed the paddock gate, he was near to tears.

*   *   *

Because he believed that a full stomach made an operation difficult, Bill had eaten no breakfast. He visualised himself meeting with an accident in the hunting-field and liked to be prepared for the worst.

"What a morning!" he sighed now, meeting Bruce in the kennel-yard. "You see, there won't be a bit of scent, not a bit."

Together they put the hounds they were taking into one court.

"Shouldn't think there'll be many out to-day," Bruce said.

The wind blew round the kennels in short, angry gusts.

"Let's hope his lordship's on time," Bill remarked, alluding to Captain Freemantle.

In the stables old Sam, groom to the Hunt for twenty-five seasons, finished plaiting Toby, a big, good-natured, deep chestnut hunter with terrific hocks and knees. "There you are. Now behave yourself," Sam said, slapping the chestnut's rump affectionately.

Tom, the stable boy, reached up to bridle little brown Prudence. "Whoa, there, whoa," he said, grasping her firmly by an ear. In the next loose-box Grey Dawn stood ready, elegant in a blue and red rug which covered her glistening saddle. She wore an egg-butt snaffle with a single plaited rein. In her eyes shone the wisdom culled from seven seasons with the Flintshire.

A little farther down stood a flashy chestnut gelding with a star and race, a snip between his nostrils and two white socks. Already he was sweating. He always recognised a hunting-morning. He was Captain Freemantle's Fearless. He wore a double bridle, and a running martingale, which was attached to the curb rein. With his lower lip he played nervously with the lip strap. There was no wisdom or content in his large eyes, only anxiety.

"Ready, Tom?" Sam called, leading out the chestnut. "It's time."

"Yeah, near enough," Tom called, buckling the throat lash.

As Bill mounted Toby the rain stopped. He thought, that's better, but I wish the wind would drop. At the same moment Captain Freemantle drove into the yard in his Sunbeam Talbot. Stepping on to the gravel, feeling the perfect gentleman as he always did in his scarlet coat, his white breeches, his mahogany-topped boots and his velvet hunting cap, he called, "'Morning, Tom, 'morning, Bruce."

Bill said, "'Morning, sir." Bruce said nothing.

Presently they were all mounted, including Sam who was to ride Grey Dawn to the meet. Tom let hounds out. Bruce cried, "Hold up, there, hold up together," and rode out of the yard first, followed by Bill with hounds around his horse's heels. After him came Captain Freemantle on a stiff-backed, uneasy Fearless, and for a moment it seemed that the sun would break through the dark sky. Last of all came Sam riding Grey Dawn, and leading the Master's second horse, Minuet.

They brought poetry to the bleak road, and music with their jingling bits and stirrups and the clip clop of hoofs and the quiet sound of hounds' pads on the tarmac.

Let the wind drop. Let us find a fox and run across the vale, prayed Bill, wondering what his wife would say if he was given notice in February.

"Trot straight, will you," muttered Captain Freemantle jabbing Fearless with his spurs, turning the little chestnut's anxiety into uneasy fear.

"Hold up, hike back, hold up together," cried Bruce, as Rambler made a dash for a cottage dustbin.

I hope it doesn't rain, thought Sam, my rheumatics are awful this morning. I'm getting too old, that's what it is.

*   *   *

Mr. Jeeves slipped on his scarlet coat, filled his flask

with cherry brandy from the sideboard, picked up his sandwich case. "'Bye, darling," he called to his wife, before opening the fine Georgian front door, smelling the air as he walked to the garage, starting up his little M.G.

I hope Bill gives us a good day, he thought, turning into the road. But maybe Freemantle's right, perhaps he ought to go. It wasn't raining any more, but there was still a fiendish wind. There won't be any scent anyway, and the ground will be impossible, he thought, passing the riding school string on their way to the meet, thinking, that fair girl sits well on her thoroughbred.

*   *   *

In Betchley a crowd was collecting. There was an air of expectancy as people waited for the first riders and the first glimpse of hounds. Women put down their umbrellas. The fishmonger watched anxiouly; last year hounds had emptied his slabs of fish.

At last in the distance they heard hoofs and cries of, "Hold up there." "Here they come," someone said.

CHAPTER THREE

THE TRUMANS arrived first.

"I knew we would be early," Jean said.

"There are a lot of people, aren't there?" Harriet cried, watching the crowd slowly swell before her eyes.

"What about a drink?" Professor Truman asked his wife.

Tony came next, cool and self-possessed, sitting beautifully on her gay, brown Southwind.

"Good morning," she called to the Trumans, and tried to remember the children's Christian names without succeeding. Are they Janet and Jean or Joan and Janet? she thought with a sense of failure, riding Southwind up and down the cobbled market-place.

Clattering into Betchley came Angela on a sweating Moonlight. A mile back she had seen a clock in a window which said eleven. Now she glanced round the market-place and with a sigh of relief saw that hounds hadn't yet arrived.

"Hallo," she called, riding towards the Trumans. "I thought I was late but now I find I'm not after all."

Mr. Jeeves parked his car, nodded to everyone and slipped into the Coach and Horses for a drink.

Into the market-place came the riding school string, first Jane, because Trooper wouldn't walk at all, but least of all behind the others; then Mrs. Pierce, a formidable figure in her black hunting-kit, white tie and bowler. Last of all Adam, who looked untidy whatever he wore, but who was grinning happily and looked the gayest of them all.

Jane didn't notice anyone as she rode through the crowd. She thought, I knew a twisted snaffle would be no good on Trooper, I shall probably break my neck to-day. Why must people want horses hunted when they're not ready to hunt?

I must keep out of the Master's way to-day, thought Adam, who had been yelled at the week before. It would be awful if he said, "I'm sick of you, Adam Clarke. You're never to come out with the Flintshire again." For a moment the smile left Adam's face; then he saw Angela, and calling, "Hallo," smiled again. Lucy and Graham talked merrily together. It was their first experience of hunting.

Then hounds came, a gay smiling bevy of black, tan

The Meet

and white, and for a moment the sun broke through the clouds and shone on the scarlet coats, brass buttons, the horn between Bill's buttons, the bits, rings, buckles, stirrups and spurs.

"Aren't they lovely?" someone cried.

Rambler made a dash for the fishmonger's, Captain Freemantle tried to crack his whip, caught it in Fearless's tail and stood helpless. Bill rode on into the market-place behind Bruce, while a policeman held up the traffic. Sam sent on Rambler. The crowd surged forward.

Someone brought Bruce and Bill a drink. Sam started walking his two horses up and down. Captain Freemantle dismounted and feeling stupid and undignified untangled his whip from Fearless's tail.

More riders began to arrive. Mr. Jeeves mounted Grey Dawn. Captain Freemantle sipped his second gin and Italian.

Mrs. Truman said, "It looks as though they're going to move off in a minute," and pulled up her girths. Angela talked to Eileen who had come on a bicycle. Adam ate one of his sandwiches and wiped his spectacles with his handkerchief. The sun went in and the wind seemed to settle in the east.

As hounds moved off, John arrived hot and flustered on a sweating Quickstep. He felt untidy and was sure he had forgotten something, though he knew he hadn't. Looking at Tony he thought, I couldn't possibly ask her to tea. Why did I ever think I could?

*   *   *

Four miles away, Mark was bicycling along wet roads. Every few moments he stopped to ask, "Have you seen a small roan pony, please?" The lump seemed to grow

25

larger in his throat, as he heard a church clock strike eleven and for a moment he wondered if he was going to cry. But he thought, I'm eleven, and boys don't cry when they're eleven, and stopped and blew his nose. Then he mounted his bicycle and rode on again.

*   *   *

An icy wind blew across the vale, numbing Angela's already cold hands, making Trooper buck and throw his head about more than ever, so that Jane lost a stirrup and her hat fell forward over her eyes.

Hounds were to draw a spinney of firs. Bill sent Bruce to watch the far side. Captain Freemantle had already disappeared as was his habit. "I'll watch this side for you," Sam told Bill. "That blighter's no use at all."

Quietly Bill put hounds in. Farther down the field waited. Adam trying not to talk, Jean forgetting and chattering in a shrill voice to Angela. Tony reciting the *Ode to a Nightingale* to herself, not hearing John's timid "Good morning." Jane still nursing her grievance. Harriet, watching the covert with wide open eyes. Mrs. Pierce discussing scenting conditions in undertones with the Master. Professor and Mrs. Truman watchful and silent. Other people talking quietly, walking their horses up and down.

Bill blew a short toot on his horns. Horses pricked their ears.

*   *   *

The seventh person Mark asked, an old man with a tawny sheep dog at his heels, said, "Yes, I've seen your pony, son. Down at the market gardens she was an hour back." Mark felt hope come back. His weariness left him. 'Which market garden?" he cried.

The old man directed him. He flung his bicycle into the ditch and ran across two fields. Suddenly he was tireless. He thought, I may be in time yet. They must be just drawing the first covert. Soon he was calling, "Merrylegs, Merrylegs." But when he came to the market garden there was no roan pony among the brussels sprouts, the celery and the artichokes. He stood forlornly for a moment; then he saw someone moving outside a greenhouse. A moment later he was asking a tall man with spectacles, "Have you seen a roan pony, please?"

He noticed the scowl then on the man's face. "Yes. And I chased it out into the road. People should keep their livestock under control," he said.

Mark felt an empty feeling right down in the pit of his stomach then. He thought of Merrylegs colliding with a lorry on the high road. Suddenly he began to cry. "That wasn't a very nice thing to do, sir," he said.

He walked blindly back across the two fields, thinking, there's no hope now. He saw, in his imagination, hounds hunting across the vale, an enormous field galloping in pursuit. He climbed a gate into the road and then he saw Merrylegs peacefully grazing not ten yards from his bicycle. For a moment he couldn't believe his eyes. Then he said, "Merrylegs, co'op Merrylegs," and took from his pocket the crust of bread, and felt his heart lift and thought, "We may still be in time. They may run this way."

*　　*　　*

In the spinney a hound spoke. Mrs. Pierce and Mr. Jeeves stopped talking. Jane said, "Ssh," to Angela and

27

Jean a fraction of a second before the Master glared at them. Adam thought, not me this time. Harriet whispered, "Do you think they've found, Mummy?" Trooper started to throw his head about. Bill blew a short toot on his horn.

On the far side of the covert Bruce watched a large dog fox emerge silently into the open. Prudence pricked her ears and started to tremble with excitement. Bruce waited until the fox had crossed the first of the open fields; then he stood in his stirrups, holloaed, and galloped to where he had last seen the fox. He stood there waving his hunting-cap and cheering hounds on as they came through the covert.

"They've found!" cried Mr. Jeeves galloping towards a cut and laid fence. Blowing the *gone away* and cheering his hounds, Bill galloped through the spinney and put Toby at a post and rail fence. Perhaps this is it. Perhaps we'll have the run of the season, he thought, but doubted it, because of the wind and the ground which was still as hard as a brick underneath and as slippery as a skating-rink on top. Toby skidded, got right under the fence and then jumped. Bill patted him as they landed safely on the other side. There'll be some broken necks by the end of to-day, he thought. In front old Thunder and Rambler had already picked up the line. Bruce was galloping on with them, keeping to the downwind side. Ahead lay the vale, grey and bleak, now that the sun had gone. Already Bill could hear the wind howling across the open fields, nothing else seemed to move; only that and his hounds and Bruce.

*   *   *

Grey Dawn took the hedge slowly and landed well into the next field. John followed and Quickstep jumped neatly like a little cat. Mrs. Pierce and Tony took it together;

28

Jane followed with her heart in her mouth, felt Trooper lengthen his stride, take off early, but still land well out into the next field.

"Well done, Jane," Mrs. Pierce called, looking back over her shoulder.

With flapping arms and legs and his heart already on the other side, Adam rode Sandy at the hedge. And Adam's determination affected Sandy, who had never jumped so high before; with a sudden spurt the dun pony jumped, scraped the top with his knees and was over. Behind him Angela, riding a sweating Moonlight, cheered. Professor and Mrs. Truman followed. Moonlight refused. Mrs. Truman called, "Go round with Angela, Harriet." Black Knight took the hedge in his stride, other horses followed.

"Come on, Harriet. We'll find a gate," Angela said.

"Can we come too?" asked Graham and Lucy, who hadn't even attempted the hedge.

Hounds ran close together in full cry, their music thrown all ways by the wind. John thought, this is heaven, as he galloped beside Tony, Quickstep's effortless stride beneath him, the wind stinging his face and the cry of hounds in his ears.

Leaning forward, standing in her stirrups, Tony was quoting Whyte-Melville as she crossed the vale:

O'er the open still careering,
Fence and furrow freely clearing,
Like the winds of heaven leaving little trace of where we pass;
With that merry music ringing,
Father Time is surely flinging
Golden sand about the moments as he shakes them from the glass;
Horn and hound are chiming gladly,
Horse and man are vying madly
In the glory of the gallop. Forty minutes on the grass!

She jumped some rails, turned left when she saw a wire fence, smiled at John and saw that there was no one in front of them save the hunt staff and Mr. Jeeves.

Sandy refused the rails. "Take him round," called Mrs. Pierce passing Adam on her grey.

Adam swore under his breath, tried again, thought, that's the end of my day, saw Angela in the distance opening a gate and galloped towards her.

Harriet said, "We've lost them, haven't we? We'll never catch them now. Oh, if only Melody would have jumped the hedge."

Angela wished Harriet would stop talking, but was too good-natured to say so. Moonlight pushed the gate open with his nose; then she saw Adam and turned in her saddle to yell, "Gate," before she galloped on across the windswept vale.

Jean fell off at the rails and watched Black Knight gallop away pursued by her parents. Now I've spoilt their day as well as mine, she thought disconsolately. Why did I have to fall off? She felt a fool walking after hounds across the vale. A straggler called, "Bad luck," as he galloped past. In the distance she could see Sam sending on the tail hounds.

*   *   *

Captain Freemantle paid for his double whisky, put out his cigarette and mounted Fearless. Can't hear a thing. Wonder where they've got to now? he thought, trotting away from the Six Horse Shoes along the main Betchley-London road.

*   *   *

With her heart in her mouth, Jane jumped the rails.

Trooper was going better now, but you still couldn't tell how he was going to jump, and he had no experience to help him cope with the difficult ground. Jane knew the fences which lay ahead—a hedge with a drop, rails on a bank, a battered gate, a stile set in a wire fence. She hated the wind. Why can't it stop? she thought. You can't hear a thing. I wish hounds would leave the vale. I wish I was on an experienced hunter. I wish I had never agreed to work for the Pierces, she thought desperately, seeing the hedge with the drop a bare thirty yards away, feeling Trooper snatch at the reins.

*　　*　　*

They're running like smoke. No one can say they aren't fit, Bill thought, watching hounds with a loving eye, slowing down Toby as he saw the hedge and drop ahead, thinking, if we kill to-day, if they run like this for forty minutes, no one can give me the sack then.

*　　*　　*

"I wonder where that blighter is," muttered Bruce, alluding to Captain Freemantle, with one eye on hounds and the other on the approaching hedge.

*　　*　　*

"Good little Merrylegs," Mark said, slipping the halter over her neat Welsh ears, whistling as he picked up his bicycle, thinking, I may be in time yet.

Ten minutes later, as he was saddling her, while his mother stood watching him with sandwiches and his gloves in her hand, Be careful now, Mark," she said.

31

"Your father says the ground's awful. Don't you go jumping to-day."

"I'll be careful," Mark promised, taking the sandwiches, putting on his gloves, thinking, I'll be lucky if I find them at all with the wind that's blowing.

"And don't be too late," his mother called as he rode away, feeling like a king on his little roan pony.

* * *

"Oh, I wish I was hunting," Anne told Ursula for the sixth time. "What are you going to do now?"

"Get the lunch," Ursula answered.

"Well, afterwards I shall go for a walk and see if I can hear hounds. They might run this way, you never know," said Anne.

The kitchen was full of buckets of bran. Anne was grating carrots.

"Lot's of people don't approve of bran mashes, you know," she told Ursula. "They act as a laxative. I think the horses might be better with a gruel each, but Mummy doesn't think so. What do you think?"

"I expect your mother knows best," Ursula answered.

* * *

They're going all right to-day. They're certainly fit, Mr. Jeeves thought, watching his hounds with pride. Smart can't be so bad after all. But where's Freemantle?

* * *

Hounds ran on across the open vale, while storm clouds

gathered in the grey sky. Thunder had dropped back. A couple and a half of third-year hounds were leading the pack. Far behind them was the faint sound of hoofs on the greasy, treacherous ground.

*   *   *

"You go first if you want to," said chivalrous John, as he and Tony approached the hedge with the drop. "Or would you rather I did? It's a nasty place."

"I've jumped it before. I'll take it slowly," Tony said, changing Southwind's gallop to a canter. "The ground's frightful, isn't it? I wish this wind would drop." Southwind jumped the hedge carefully. Quickstep followed. "Thank goodness that's behind us," John said.

"It'll probably stop a few," Tony remarked. "I like your mare. What's she called?"

"Quickstep. She's eight. Dad bought her at a sale. He's got quite an eye for a horse. He used to ride himself when he was younger."

"Daddy always gets Carlton-Smith to find mine," Tony said, naming a well-known dealer. "But when I grow out of Southwind I want an Irish horse. I shall go to the Dublin Show and choose him myself."

"Mrs. Pierce is going well," John said, looking back over his shoulder. "I wonder what the fair girl's like on the big horse."

"I shouldn't want to be her. He looks a difficult horse to ride," Tony remarked.

"I think he's a young one," John said. Together they galloped on towards the rails on the bank. Ahead were only hounds, Bill and Bruce and the Master.

"This is the best run we've had for seasons," Tony said.

*   *   *

Trooper took the hedge much too fast. Jane fell forward as he landed and lost her hat. He pecked, regained his balance and they galloped on leaving the hat lost and forlorn on the short wet grass.

* * *

Angela couldn't hear anything. I wish the huntsman would blow his horn more often; I'm sure the other one did, she thought.

"Have we lost them? Where do you think they are?" Harriet asked.

"I don't know," Angela replied, trying not to sound cross.

"What a pity," Lucy remarked.

"My legs are aching," Graham said.

In front was a wire fence. "We'd better turn right," Angela said.

"Hi, wait for me," Adam cried, slowly gaining on Angela and her party.

"I think I'm going home. I'm freezing. What about you, Lucy?" Graham asked.

"I don't know. Do you think you know the way?" Lucy replied doubtfully.

"We'll soon find it," Graham replied with confidence, kicking Jumbo in the ribs, turning him round. "After all, we've got tongues in our heads."

"Gosh, you are feeble," Harriet cried, watching them ride back across the vale.

* * *

"Thanks awfully, Mummy," Jean said, taking Black Knight from her mother. "I'm sorry to be such a nuisance."

"Everybody falls off sometimes. It'll probably be me next time," Professor Truman said.

"I think we'd better go round that awful hedge with a drop, don't you?" Mrs. Truman asked her husband.

"I hope Harriet's all right," she added a moment later.

"She's with the Clavers' girl, isn't she?" the professor asked. "I expect she'll be all right with her."

*　　　*　　　*

On second thoughts Jane rode back for her hat. She dismounted and discovered that her legs were wobbly. I wish I had brought my sandwiches, she thought.

It was some moments before she managed to remount Trooper; he twirled round and round, caught his reins in his stirrups, trod on Jane's toe and banged her head with his. But at last she was back in the saddle and, galloping on towards the rails and bank, with no one behind and about twelve members of the field strung out in front. Sue suddenly remembered Graham and Lucy then, and, with a queer sick feeling wondered whether it had been her job to look after them. But Mrs. Pierce never said anything, she thought, already on the defensive. How could I anyway when I was riding a young horse? And now suddenly the rails were in front of her and she realised that she was going much too fast. "Steady, steady, Trooper," she said, snatching at the reins. But it's too late to do anything, she thought, as the big thoroughbred lengthened his stride. He took off and she heard a splitting noise as he hit the rails. She tried to clutch his mane, felt him stumble against the bank, shut her eyes, thought, thank goodness I went back for my hat, felt his knees go under him, thought, he's falling, what will the Pierces say? Something hit her head. There seemed a great weight on her legs. Then everything went black.

Something hit her head

36

CHAPTER FOUR

GALLOPING ALONG the grass verge on the Betchley-London road, Mark saw Captain Freemantle ahead and was suddenly filled with hope.

"Perhaps I'm going to find them after all, he thought happily, urging Merrylegs faster. They can't be far away if he's here. As he drew near, he changed Merrylegs's gallop to a walk, and listened intently for the horn. Then he looked at Captain Freemantle and saw that he was listening too and had that distracted appearance people get when they've lost hounds.

But he can't have, he thought, after all, he's a whip.

For a time Mark followed Captain Freemantle up and down the London road, then he summoned his courage and said, "Do you know where they are, sir?"

Captain Freemantle turned in his saddle. He thought, thank goodness it's only a small boy.

"No, I lost them half an hour ago. My horse fell at some rails," he lied.

Mark thought, that's funny. Why hasn't he got any mud on his coat? "I think I'll push on," he said, galloping away down the road, thinking, hounds may be in the next county by now.

*   *   *

Hounds left the vale. Still in full cry, still bunched together they ran towards Betchley Park.

*   *   *

Prudence was tiring. Her neck was white with sweat, mud and sweat clung to her sides. She was sobbing for breath. Bruce halted and thought, I'll let her get her second wind. He could see the house which belonged to Betchley Park, standing on its hill. It was a monster of a house, huge, hideously built by a man who had made his money in the Gold Rush and came back to England to spend it. Only one old lady lived there now and threequarters of the rooms were shuttered.

I hope they don't run into the park, Bruce thought, the old girl's anti-sports and then there's the deer. He saw Bill approaching and waited for him.

"Just letting the mare get her second wind," he called, patting Prudence.

"Can't say they aren't running to-day," Bill called back with satisfaction in his voice. "We'd better try and keep them out of the park though. If my second whip was any good, he'd be down there on that road," he added.

"Not much hope of that," Bruce replied. They galloped on together, and, because the wind was blowing the cry of the pack all ways, Bill blew his horn at intervals to let the field know just where they were.

*   *   *

"But we can't jump that," Adam cried, looking at the rails and bank. "It's much too difficult."

"I know, I'm looking for a way round," Angela replied. It was Harriet who saw Jane and Trooper.

"Look, look, there's something on the other side," she cried.

"Where?" asked Angela, and then she saw a horse staggering to his feet, and a bowler hat lying a few yards from the far side of the bank.

"Gosh, there's been an accident. How awful!" she cried.

38

"I wonder who it is," said Adam, who was short-sighted and hadn't yet identified Trooper.

Angela didn't answer. She was already galloping towards the bank. Once there she flung Moonlight's reins to Harriet, and scrambled over to the far side. She saw a crumpled heap and fair hair. "It's Jane," she cried.

Because suddenly everything seemed so awful, Harriet began to cry. Dismounting, leaving Sandy to his own devices, Adam clambered over the bank and under the broken rail.

"Is she dead?" he asked.

"No, but she's unconscious," Angela replied, feeling Jane's heart.

It was then that Adam noticed Trooper standing dejectedly with blood pouring from a gashed forearm. "Trooper's hurt too. Oh gosh, what shall we do?" he asked.

Angela was remembering her first aid, Already she had her coat off. "I'll see to Jane. You see to him," she said.

Secretly Adam hated the sight of blood, but now was no time to think of that. "Poor old Trooper," he said, patting the big horse's wet neck, looking at the blood staining the grass red, thinking, it looks like blood from an artery.

"Staunch the blood with your hunting-tie, if it's clean. Pack the wound with it," Angela advised, putting her coat over Jane, thinking, we need an ambulance, looking round for a house but seeing none.

Adam's hands were trembling. It was with difficulty that he unpinned his hunting-tie. "We need an ambulance," Angela said. "I think she may be badly hurt."

She felt calm and was surprised to find that her teeth were chattering. What can we do? I wish some grownups would come, she thought. "Can you see anyone, Harriet?" she called.

"No, no one," Harriet said. "What's the matter? Is she badly hurt?"

"I don't know," Angela said and the seriousness in her voice frightened Harriet. "She's not dead, is she?" Harriet asked.

"No, I expect she's broken something," Angela replied, trying to sound calm and matter of fact.

"You'd better go for an ambulance," she told Adam. "I'll look after Trooper," she added, thinking, there's nothing more I can do for Jane. I daren't move her in case she's broken her back.

"I think he's cut an artery," said Adam, who had his coat off and was tearing up his shirt, quite oblivious of the piercing wind. "It looks pretty bad anyway."

"If you ride towards the big road you must come to a house soon," Angela said, taking bits of his shirt from Adam.

"Can't I do anything?" cried Harriet.

"I'll be as quick as I can," Adam promised, putting on his coat.

Angela packed Trooper's wound with the bits of Adam's shirt, then she bound it with his hunting-tie.

Adam scrambled back over the bank.

"What's she like? And what's happened to Trooper?" Harriet asked with tears streaming down her face.

"Jane's unconscious. I think Trooper's all right," But is he, Adam thought, catching Sandy, mounting, riding away across the vale. Supposing he bleeds to death? Supposing he's severed a tendon? He may have to be destroyed. He looked across the open vale and looked in vain for telegraph posts or any sign of a road. With panic in his heart, he thought, I'm lost and Jane may be dying back there by the bank.

Holding Trooper, realising that she was cold, Angela thought, I hope Adam hurries. I wish someone else would

40

come. I wish I had some hot tea to give Jane if she comes round.

"Why didn't you let me go with Adam?" Harriet called, still crying on the other side.

*   *   *

The Trumans had lost hounds, but it wasn't that they were worrying about, it was Harriet.

"Oh, I hope she's all right," Mrs. Truman said. "I can't think why we ever let her go off by herself."

"But she's with Angela," Jean replied.

"She was, you mean," Mrs. Truman said.

"There seems to be a mist coming up," Professor Truman remarked, "and that's not going to help anyone."

*   *   *

"I thought you knew the way, Graham," Lucy said. "You said you did."

"It's this mist coming up. It makes everything seem so queer," Graham complained.

"I think we're riding in a circle. I'm sure that's the fence we passed five minutes ago."

"Let's stop and get our bearings," Graham suggested.

"If we can. Personally, I'm completely lost," Lucy said.

*   *   *

"They seem to be running towards Betchley Park, don't they? That's a curse, isn't it?" Tony said.

"You mean Miss What's-her-name's anti-blood sports?" John asked.

"Yes, very much so. She'll probably chase us with broomsticks," Tony replied laughing.

"I wonder where everyone else is. There doesn't seem to be anyone behind. Even Jane's disappeared," John said.

"The wind's dropped, that's something. At least we can hear hounds," Tony remarked.

"But the light's so eerie. I believe there's a mist coming up," John said.

Their horses were beginning to tire. Together they jumped the awkward stile, turned left when they saw a wire fence ahead.

"This is a marvellous run. I am enjoying myself. Aren't you?" Tony said.

"Yes, like anything," John replied.

*　　*　　*

They're running towards the park and it's alive with deer. I hope to goodness Freemantle's down on the main road, Mr. Jeeves thought. And where's Sam? Poor Dawn's all done in. He jumped a rickety gate; thought, there's a mist or something coming up. That's going to make a mess of things.

*　　*　　*

Mrs. Pierce's big grey was lame. He had slipped as she put him at the battered gate and though he had landed quite safely, he was limping after a few yards. There was nothing she could do but walk him home, and where was Jane? she wondered, and Adam, Graham and Lucy? As long as they're all together, they'll be all right, she thought; and if Harold's back from the sale, he can fetch me in the trailer. But all the same she was worried. Disaster seemed to hang over everything, and she couldn't see far because of the mist which was stealing across the vale. I'd better try and find a kiosk, she thought, feeling in her pocket to see whether she had change—what an awful day!

* * *

"He would run that way," Bruce grumbled, turning up the collar of his scarlet coat as he galloped, because suddenly he was cold.

"And look at the mist. We shan't be able to see a thing soon," Bill said.

"I expect Freemantle's sitting by a fire somewhere," Bruce said.

"Or on his way home," Bill added bitterly. They galloped on in silence across the fields, silent but for the cry of hounds.

* * *

"I've lost them, that's all there is to it," Sam muttered to himself as he jogged along a country road. If I don't hear them in another ten minutes I'm going home, he decided. Shan't be able to see a thing soon with this mist coming up anyway, and the damp's not doing my rheumatics any good. He thought of his little house by the kennels, of a warm cup of tea and something cooked; of the range glowing in the kitchen and his wife saying "Well, what sort of day did you have, Sam?" and in his imagination he replied, "Blooming awful."

He stopped to listen again and thought, I'm too old for this job, that's what it is.

* * *

Anne said, "That was a jolly good omelette, Ursula. I wish I could cook like you do. I'm going out to listen now. You never know, they might run this way."

"Here, put your coat on," Ursula called, running after her, "and don't go far."

* * *

Mark thought, I can hear them. They're running this way, and his heart gave a great leap of joy. "We've found them after all," he said, leaning forward to pat Merrylegs's neck. Then he heard the horn and he thought, that isn't the *gone away* the huntsman's blowing, it's *long leave the covert*, or *Home*. It must be later than I thought, he decided, suddenly feeling sick with disappointment. They must have decided to call it a day. And I've been rushing about the countryside for nothing. For a moment he considered turning for home, then he thought, I may as well wait and see what happens.

* * *

An escaped deer jumped up in front of hounds and made straight for the park, and with one accord the pack left the fox they'd been hunting, and, still in full cry, followed the line of the deer.

* * *

Two fields behind Bill said, "They've changed. You can hear it by their cry. They're on a deer now."

Bruce didn't speak. He thought, now we're in for it. Everyone knows the park's out of bounds for hunting. Poor Bill will be in deep water for it—he never has any luck.

Bill took the horn from between his buttons and blew, *Home, home. Long leave the covert.*

Bruce called, "Heel away bike home, home." Why did

I ever come to the Flintshire? Why didn't I stay as first whip to the Melville? Bill thought, there'll be the devil to pay if they get in the park.

*　　*　　*

No good going on, Captain Freemantle thought, hounds can't do much with this mist coming up. I may as well turn for home, he decided, thinking of tea with his wife in front of the drawing-room fire, and a whisky afterwards and a long hot bath.

He lit a cigarette and rode back along the road to where he had last seen a signpost. Fearless hurried, guessing his rider's decision, already thinking of the feed awaiting him and the deep bed of straw, which he had left so reluctantly in the morning.

*　　*　　*

Harriet was still crying. "You ought to have let me go with him, Angela," she called. "I'm sure he's lost."

"It's too late now to cry over spilt milk," Angela replied, near to tears herself.

Her hands were cold and though Trooper's wound had stopped bleeding he looked miserable and was shivering from head to foot. I'd better lead him up and down, she thought, but when she tried she found he could barely hobble. Jane looked ghastly lying beneath the bank, her face was ashen and though she was unconscious, she seemed to be shivering. Oh hurry, Adam, hurry, Angela prayed. And then, but supposing Harriet's right, supposing he is lost? She began to cry then. She thought, this is like a nightmare, but it's true, that's what, so awful.

*　　*　　*

If only I could find a road, Adam thought desperately. Or a house, anything. But I can't see a thing with this mist coming down. He stopped and wiped his spectacles, but it didn't make any difference. He thought of Jane lying by the bank, and started to gallop madly hither and thither, calling, "Hoi, help! Anyone about? There's been an accident."

*   *   *

"We'll never find her now," Mrs. Truman said.

"Maybe she's raced home," Jean suggested hopefully.

"I don't think that's likely. Knowing Harriet, I'm sure she'll stay out to the bitter end," Professor Truman replied.

"If she's with Angela and the riding-school children, they'll see her back," said Mrs. Truman doubtfully.

Slowly, disconsolately, they turned for home.

*   *   *

But it wasn't a mist which blotted out the vale. Treacherously, with startling rapidity a fog descended over everything, obliterating all, until visibility was nil, and hounds hunted like a ghost pack across the disastrous vale.

CHAPTER FIVE

HOUNDS' CRY came muffled through the fog to Mark, still standing on the main road. They are running directly towards me, he thought, and then realised that behind him was the park and in the park was the famous herd of Japanese deer. I must stop them, he thought, but how when he couldn't even see them he couldn't imagine.

Then he remembered the gates by the lodge. I'll shut them, he thought, already cantering down the road.

He threw his reigns over some palings and pulled frantically at the heavy gates, hung on pillars topped by lions, and slowly inch by inch they began to move. He felt like cheering them. He could still hear hounds and, farther away, the huntsman desperately blowing the horn.

As the gates closed and Mark latched them, he was filled with a great sense of achievement. His awful morning didn't seem to matter now, nor the knowledge that he had probably missed the run of the season.

Whistling, *My Bonnie lies over the Ocean*, he patted Merrylegs and remounted.

The huntsman will be pleased, he thought, and won't I have something to tell them when I get home.

Hounds were coming nearer each moment, but he still couldn't see them because of the fog. What a day! he thought, I hope Mum isn't worrying.

*　　*　　*

Where am I? What's happened? Jane thought opening her eyes, seeing a dumpy figure which must be Angela and a large horse which she supposed was Trooper. Her head ached and she couldn't remember anything which had happened after riding to the meet.

She carefully focused her eyes on Angela and said, "Is it Monday or Tuesday?" and then, "What's the time?"

Angela was surprised. She hadn't expected Jane to come round until she was safely and comfortably installed in a hospital bed. She said, "It's Thursday. I think it's about three o'clock. How do you feel?"

"Awful," Jane replied, and was violently sick.

"You'd better stay where you are," Angela told her. "Keep my coat over you. There's an ambulance coming." Jane didn't seem to hear her. She said, "Sorry, I've forgotten; did you say it was Monday or Tuesday and what's the time?"

"It's Thursday, and I suppose about three o'clock," Angela replied patiently, thinking, I wish Adam would hurry up.

"Has she come round?" cried Harriet, suddenly appearing on top of the bank. "It's all right, I've tied up the horses. How do you feel, Jane?" she shrieked.

"Ssh," said Angela.

"Who's that?" said Jane, sitting up. "What's happened to Graham and Lucy and Adam? Where's Mrs. Pierce? What's happened to Trooper?"

"It's Harriet. Graham and Lucy have gone home. Adam's getting you an ambulance. We don't know where Mrs. Pierce is," Angela said.

Jane thought that over for a bit. Then she said, "Is Trooper hurt? How did it happen? Is there a fog or is it my eyesight?"

"Trooper's staked himself and is slightly lame," said Angela, thinking, that's a white lie so it doesn't matter. "We weren't here so we don't know how it happened, and there's a perfectly awful fog. Now try and rest. You've hit your head and talking won't do you any good," Angela finished, sounding like a nurse.

"Oh, I hope Trooper isn't badly hurt," Jane said a moment later. "The Pierces will be awfully upset. He's worth an awful lot of money."

"He'll be all right," Angela replied in soothing tones. "The ambulance will be here presently."

I don't want an ambulance, Jane thought, moving her legs, finding they worked and so did her back. If only I didn't feel in such a muddle, she thought, and my shoulder feels awfully funny. I wonder what the Pierces will say about Trooper. I wonder why he fell. I wish I could remember more.

Jane looks awful. Harriet thought. I wish there were

48

some grown-ups here. Angela's all right, but she's not like a grown-up.

I wish Adam would come back. I wish Trooper would stop shivering. Why didn't I tell Adam to ring up the Pierces at the same time for a trailer? Angela thought. And then supposing he can't find us again when he has got an ambulance . . . ? I mustn't panic. Everything will turn out all right in the end—it always does.

*   *   *

Sam turned into the stableyard.

"Hallo, you're early," Tom called, coming out of one of the boxes. In the kennels the hounds who had been left behind heard hoofs and started to sing.

"I lost them at twelve o'clock. Then this fog came down, didn't seem much point in staying out after that," Sam said, slipping to the ground.

"I expect they'll be back soon anyway," Tom said, whistling cheerfully, thinking, we'll get finished early to-night; I'll have time to slip down to the pub for a game of darts."

"Well they can't do much in this. You can't see a yard in front of your nose," Sam said.

*   *   *

It seems so potty to get lost when you're only a field or two from your own house, Anne thought, walking desperately in circles. And poor Ursula will be getting frantic. If I walk dead straight I'm sure to meet something soon.

*   *   *

"Gosh, this is awful. I can't see a thing. Can you hear anything, John?" Tony asked.

"They're running towards the park still. We'd better hurry, Bill and Bruce will need all the people they can get if hounds start hunting deer," John replied.

"Ware hole," Tony yelled a moment later, "and I think there's another wire fence ahead."

"This place is like a bird cage," John called back. "I wish we were allowed to carry wire cutters."

"We'll have to go back and see it we can find a gate," Tony said presently, looking at the long unbroken wire fence.

"We'll never get to the road in time now," John said. "I only hope hounds don't get killed as they go across."

They galloped back across the enormous field they were in, and eventually they found a gate. But someone had passed that way before them and, leaving the gate wide open, had let a large herd of cattle on to the plough beyond.

John stared at the cattle lumbering over the furrows in the fog. "That's why farmers object to hunting," he said in furious tones. "We'll have to stay now and get them back."

"But we can't. What about the deer? They're much more important," Tony replied.

"No, they're not. This looks like Tom Rodger's accredited herd, and that's more valuable than any amount of deer," John said, already starting to ride outside the cattle, which Tony could see now were Guernseys.

"It's not just the deer; it's the hunt too. Miss What's-her-name will take it to court, if anything happens to one of her precious deer," she said, looking at John with large brown eyes.

We're going to quarrel in a moment, John thought. What an awful day this is. "But we'd be too late to do anything about the wretched deer now anyway," he answered. "And for all we know there's dozens of people on the road already."

"Well, I'm going down there anyway," Tony said, and thinking, what harm can a few cows come to on a ploughed field? She galloped away to where she guessed the road lay.

And that's that, John thought, I shall never be able to ask her to tea now. But I couldn't have galloped on and left Tom Rodger's herd roaming loose around the countryside, because for all I know this field isn't fenced at all.

Quickstep stumbled wearily over the furrows, and every moment the day seemed bleaker and the cattle more numerous as John with an aching heart pursued them through the thickening fog.

*   *   *

Mrs. Pierce led her limping grey hunter on to a winding country road. There must be a kiosk somewhere, she thought, even in these rural parts. Then she heard hoofs and thought, perhaps that's Jane and the children and her sinking spirits lifted a little. A moment later the Trumans came into sight, waving madly. "Hi," they called. "We've lost Harriet. Have you seen her by any chance?"

"She couldn't get over the hedge," Jean explained, halting Black Knight. "She went round with two of your pupils and Angela Clavers."

"And we haven't seen her since," Mrs. Truman added.

"You look in trouble too. Is your horse lame?" Professor Truman asked.

"Yes, he is, unfortunately," Mrs. Pierce replied, "and I'm afraid I've no idea where your daughter is. I'm hoping my pupils are with my girl groom. Have you any idea where I can find a telephone?"

"None whatsoever. I'm afraid we're completely lost," Professor Truman replied.

"What a disastrous day it is," Mrs. Truman remarked.

Jean was near to tears. She was afraid Harriet had fallen off and hurt herself and was now lying alone in a damp field. And if I hadn't fallen off and wasted everyone's time it might never have happened, she thought, following her parents along the road, filled with hopeless remorse.

"I suppose we'll come to a house sooner or later," Mrs. Pierce said. "I want to get hold of Harold, so that he can collect this horse in a trailer."

But the Trumans didn't seem to hear her.

After a time Mrs. Truman said, "I suppose we'd better go home. She may be there by now." And when they came to a signpost they took the road which would lead them eventually to the river and the old mill.

Ten minutes later Mrs. Pierce saw the scarlet sides of a kiosk through the fog. I knew I must come to one in the end, she thought triumphantly, quickening her pace.

The big grey stood outside, pathetically resting one foreleg as she telephoned, his reigns hooked over her arm. She could hear the bell ringing at the other end, but no one answered. What can he be doing? she thought. The sale must be over by now. Presently she stepped on to the road and stood wondering what to do next. Finally, she decided to try a local horsebox man and returned to the kiosk.

*   *   *

They'll be in the park by now, Bruce thought, savagely cutting wire with his cutters, watching Bill gallop on, remounting, galloping in pursuit.

We're too late, Bill thought, putting his horn to his

parched lips, blowing, blowing, blowing, because there seemed nothing else he could do.

* * *

Mr. Jeeves was lost with the one member of the hunt he hated, Major Smith, a thickset, ex-Guards officer with a large moustache. And to-day will be the end of Freemantle, he thought furiously, trying not to hear Major Smith's ceaseless flow of talk, where is he? What's he

Wiping his spectacles for the hundredth time

doing? I haven't seen him since the meet. And where's Sam with Minuet?

"This reminds me of a day I had once with the Beaufort," Major Smith began . . .

* * *

Hours must have passed, Adam thought desperately, wiping his spectacles with his handkerchief for the hundredth time. I'm never going to find the road, he thought hopelessly, patting his weary mount's dripping neck. Darkness will come and I shall still be looking. And all the time in his mind's eye he could see Jane lying a crumpled heap by the bank, and Trooper dripping bright arterial blood on to the short, cold grass. Why did this have to happen to me? he asked, gazing into the fog and thinking, I'm probably riding in circles. Presently he decided to let Sandy find the way, and dropping the reins sat still and waited.

For a time the dun pony stood dejectedly and then life seemed to come back to his tired limbs and he set off with a purposeful stride in the one direction Adam had doubted from the beginning.

* * *

Captain Freemantle trotted briskly into the stableyard, looking round and called, "Hi, Tom."

Sam and Tom were smoking together in the saddle room.

"He's early," Sam said.

Tom took Fearless. Captain Freemantle lit a cigarette. "Had a rotten day," he said. "Don't suppose hounds will stay out much longer—there's no scent and with this fog there'll soon be chaos."

"Where did you leave them, sir?" Tom asked.

"Haven't an idea," Captain Freemantle replied, getting into his car, starting the engine, turning on the foglight. "Jeeves will be crazy if he stays out in this," he called back over his shoulder, as he slipped in the clutch, trod on the accelerator, slid silently down the drive, thinking of tea, of taking off his boots, and of firelight shining on distempered walls.

"He's not a 'alfpence of good," Sam said. "Might as well have no whip as have him."

"You've said it," Tom replied, taking off Fearless's saddle, before rubbing him down.

Sam fetched scissors and cut out the chestnut's plaits. Together the two men looked him over for thorns.

"Doesn't look as though he's been through much mud to-day," Sam remarked.

"Why he wants to be a whip beats me," Tom said. "If he wasn't he could pub crawl all day and no one would notice."

They rugged and bandaged the chestnut, turned off the electric light and left him in peace.

"Now for a spot of tea," Sam said.

*   *   *

Here they come, thought Mark, standing alone on the road. Hounds seemed very close now, though he still couldn't see them, and Merrylegs was wildly excited. She turned round and round in the road, grabbed at the lower ring on her pelham, and dug frantically with all her hoofs at once.

Bill was still blowing the horn, and in a moment, Mark saw the first hound, and then something flashed past too large for a fox, too small for a pony, and he thought, it's a deer! He screamed, "Hold up there, hold up," galloped desperately in front of hounds now pouring through a hedge on to the road. He thought, thank goodness I shut the gates, saw the young stag jump the palings, and with a cry of anguish, hounds stream through a gap into the park beyond. He galloped down the road, pulled the heavy gates open and galloped into the park, only to discover that more palings separated him from the pack. He halted and yelled, "Heel away bike home, home, come home," into the fog and thought, why didn't I look to see whether there was a gap in the park fence? What a fool I've been!

He heard hoofs on the road and thought, that must be the huntsman and Bruce. He galloped on through the park until he found a gate, which he opened. He heard the sound of hounds crashing through bracken and their muffled cry as they put up more deer, until a whole herd seemed to be stampeding. He thought, supposing they kill? and saw in his imagination a hind with blood dripping from her throat. He remembered that the ground was treacherous with rabbit holes, and overhead boughs brushed his hat. In the distance he heard the horn and Bill calling his hounds through the fog. And now he could see the faint outline of hounds and galloping on he too called, "Home, come home, home," until all the words ran into one.

CHAPTER SIX

"WHO'S THERE?" Adam called, seeing a small figure standing still five yards away from him in the fog.

Anne thought, it's a horse; they can't have run this far. All the same she hoped they had. It would be lovely to have her parents home early, and she had been very near to tears as she stood trying desperately to get her bearings.

"It's Anne, Anne Truman," she called back. "Who art thou?"

"It's me, Adam," he said, riding to meet her, thinking, thank goodness I've found help at last.

"There's been a terrible accident," he said a moment later. "I must find a telephone; it's urgent."

"Who is it?" cried Anne. "What's happened? Is it Jean?"

"No, Jane, Jane and Trooper," he replied. "They're both terribly hurt. I must find a telephone."

"But I'm lost!" Anne cried. "I came here looking for the hunt and now I can't find my way back."

Adam thought, it can't be true. She can't be lost too. It was a moment before his mind would accept the fact.

"It seems so silly," Anne said. "We can't be more than a quarter of a mile from the house, and gosh, I should know these fields, I've walked in them often enough."

"Sandy brought me here. I can't imagine why," he said.

"Where is Jane?" she asked.

"Miles away," he replied. "That's what's so terrible," and as he spoke he saw her again by the bank. "We *must* get to a telephone somehow," he said.

Anne thought for a moment. Then she said, "You know why Sandy brought you here? We hired him once for the holidays. He lived with us. Let's see if he will lead us home."

Adam dropped the reins and Sandy walked on.

"He seems to know where he's going," Anne said.

"He's been marvellous," Adam replied dismounting. "I galloped him for ages round and round in circles."

"I think I've been going in circles too," Anne replied.

Adam was beginning to feel better. Having Anne as company eased his feeling of desperation. He thought, maybe Jane isn't so ill after all, perhaps she's already better. Perhaps Mrs. Pierce has turned up now.

"Who's with her? She's not all alone, is she?" Anne asked.

"Angela and Harriet. Angela's been marvellous. People may laugh at her riding, but she's wonderful in an emergency," Adam said.

They came to a gate.

"Gosh!" Anne cried. "We're nearly home."

"Trooper must have hit the rails and then fallen. It was that awful fence on top of a bank half-way across the vale. And the ground was frightful," Adam said.

They could see the Mill House now and hear the river. They both began to run.

"I've never seen your house before," Adam said.

"Here, I'll take Sandy," Anne cried a moment later. "You run to the back door and ask Ursula to show you the telephone."

Adam didn't know who Ursula was, but he ran obediently to the back door, banged the horseshoe knocker and charged into the kitchen.

Ursula was taking cakes out of the oven.

"Quick, quick, I must ring for an ambulance," he cried.

Ursula dropped the cakes on to the brick floor.

"What's happened? Is it Anne?" she cried.

"No, a girl from the riding school," Adam replied, following her through the hall into the living-room where the telephone stood on a white window-sill. "What do I dial?" he asked, suddenly panicking.

"Me, I don't know," she said.

He dialled O and cried, "I want an ambulance," when the operator answered. There was a click and a man spoke. He wanted to know where Adam was and Adam turned to Ursula, who said "It is the Mill House. The residence of Professor Truman."

"It'll be along right away," the man said.

"But the girl isn't here. It's a riding accident," Adam cried into the receiver and realised with a feeling of horror, that he didn't know where the bank and rails were, only that they were somewhere in the vale.

"Where is she then?" the voice at the other end asked, and Adam replied, "Somewhere in the vale."

"I'm afraid that isn't much help. Can't you give more precise directions?" the man asked, and Adam could only reply, "No," and think, what a fool I've been; and felt suddenly empty inside.

"I think we'd better come to the Mill House," the man said, and rang off.

"I don't know where she is, that's the awful part," Adam cried, turning to Ursula. "I've been lost in the fog for hours."

"The vale, it is so big," Ursula said.

Anne took off Sandy's tack, put straw on his back and a rug on top. There was a haynet and water in the box. She patted him and tore indoors.

Adam was still standing by the telephone. He told her what had happened, occasionally Ursula chipped in.

"How awful! But I think I may know the way to the vale. I hunted across it last season, and I remember going round that awful fence," Anne said.

Presently they all went into the kitchen and Ursula ruefully picked up the cakes and they drank tea and waited for the ambulance. And it seemed to Adam then that the accident and the hunt had all taken place years ago. He couldn't believe that only a few hours had passed since he stood in the market-place, smiling and greeting his friends, optimistically looking forward to a run across the vale.

*   *   *

John couldn't see any more cows. He thought, that must be the lot, and shut the gate. Then he remounted and rode on across the plough.

He thought he could still hear the horn, but couldn't be sure because often his imagination would play him up and he would hear it for hours after hounds had called it a day, and even sometimes in bed, so that he would sometimes think there must be a ghost pack which hunted beneath the light of the moon.

He came to another gate and to a hedge which he jumped, and then he could hear hounds hunting in the park. So no one was in time, no one stopped them after all, he thought, and wondered whether Tony was riding with them, or had turned for home and was hacking along the main road.

He crossed another field, slid down a bank into the road, halted Quickstep and listened.

He could hear the faint cry of hounds, the crack of a whip; then an army convoy approached and their engines drowned everything else.

He found the lodge gates and entered the park. He saw fresh hoof marks on the gravelled drive. He trotted on into the depths of the park, trying to watch both the holes below and the boughs overhead.

*　　*　　*

Tony, riding slowly along the main road, thought, why did I ever leave John? He's much nicer than I ever imagined and I was too late to stop hounds anyway, just as he said I would be. She could hear hounds hunting wildly in the park, but she didn't see much point in joining the hunt staff already pursuing them through the fog.

I shall only lame Southwind, she thought, and I'm no good at hunting-noises and can't crack my whip. It would be different if I was with John. Would he come to tea if I asked him? she wondered and tried to visualise him drinking out of her mother's delicate china tea cups, which came from an expensive shop in London and were almost impossible to match. It would be better to ask him to lunch, she decided. But then what could we do all afternoon? I don't suppose he likes reading poetry or looking at pictures. She heard hoofs then and into sight came Mrs. Pierce leading her limping grey.

Oh dear, there's been an accident, Tony thought, waving to Mrs. Pierce and calling, "Are you all right?"

Mrs. Pierce had telephoned four horse box firms. Two hadn't answered and the remaining two hadn't a horse box left in their garages. When she heard hoofs coming towards her she had hoped it would be Jane. Now when she saw Tony she was disappointed. "He's sprained a tendon," she called back, "I'm slowly making my way home."

"I'm so sorry. What bad luck," Tony replied. "Isn't it an awful day? Everyone seems lost, and now hounds are hunting in the park."

"I suppose you haven't seen my girl?" Mrs. Pierce asked.

"You mean with fair hair on the big thoroughbred? No, not for hours. I think she must have come a cropper or gone home by now," Tony replied.

"She's supposed to be looking after some of my pupils," Mrs. Pierce said, "I'm really rather worried."

"If I see her I'll tell them to go then, shall I?" Tony asked.

"Thank you very much," Mrs. Pierce said.

Tony dismounted, because it seemed more polite to walk beside Mrs. Pierce than to ride. They walked on in silence.

At intervals they could hear the horn faint and muffled by the fog. Glancing at her watch, Tony saw that it was three o'clock. I shall just be home in time for tea, she thought, seeing the stable lights shining down the drive, Mundy taking Southwind, tea by the drawing-room fire and Brutus running to meet her.

Where can Harold be? and what's happened to Jane and Graham, Lucy and Adam? Mrs. Pierce asked herself, and imagined angry parents telephoning the stables for news of their children.

The road which ran alongside the park fence seemed endless. Mrs. Pierce's ancient boots were rubbing her heels, and every moment the grey seemed lamer. Tony walked on and on with a long effortless stride, and dusk seemed to fall, and suddenly there was rain in the air. And still they could hear hounds hunting half a dozen different deer with sharp, excited cries, quite unlike their usual music.

*   *   *

Mark was very near to hounds. Behind him he could hear the hunt staff galloping along the gravelled drive. Although he had failed to stop hounds entering the park, it gave him a thrill to think that he was the only person still with them. And Merrylegs was being marvellous. She had jumped dozens of holes and avoided others by split inches; she seemed as determined as Mark to stop hounds hunting deer, and as they charged under low branches, Mark with his head on her neck thought she must be one of the best hunters in the world.

And then a figure loomed up out of the fog and cried, "Hi there. What do you think you're doing? You're trespassing," and Mark saw a small slight woman brandishing a branch.

His first instinct was to flee, but he repulsed it and called back, "Trying to stop hounds, madam."

In spite of her size she looked formidable and Merrylegs shied as she approached.

"This park is private property. You will be summoned for trespassing. As for your dogs, I've roused my gamekeeper and told him to shoot at sight," she said.

Mark suddenly felt cold all over. He cried, "You can't do that. You can't shoot hounds."

He saw that she had grey hair scraped into a bun, and gooseberry eyes, and long artistic hands.

"Oh yes, I can. And what's more, I will," she said.

"Hi, there, What do you think you're doing?"

"I think it's disgusting all those dogs and men hunting one poor little fox. And now they're hunting my deer and if you think they can do that you're mistaken."

"But I'm trying to stop them. That's why I'm here," Mark said, thinking, she's mad. Oh, why doesn't someone else come?

"Well, you can go," she said. "I'll look after the dogs." And then Mark heard a shot, or what he thought afterwards might have been the crack of a whip though he was never sure, and his heart gave a great leap and he thought, they're killing them already, and he imagined hounds dropping dead in the bracken one by one.

"It's you who should go to prison," he cried, forgetting the civil tongue his father had trained him to keep in his head. "You're a murderer. Why can't you leave hounds alone?"

"Because they're hunting my deer. Now get out of the park before I call the police," she cried, waving her branch furiously.

Mark thought, I must do something, I can't just let them shoot hounds. He said, "I'm not frightened of the police. And I'm not getting out of the park until the last hound is outside with the huntsman."

Then he closed his legs against Merrylegs's sides and galloped away across the park.

*　　　*　　　*

Captain Freemantle sat sipping tea. "It was a ghastly day," he told his wife. "Hardly any scent and the ground was as slippery as the devil. I should think hounds would be home by now."

He had taken off his boots and scarlet coat and now, sitting by the fire in his bedroom slippers, he felt pleasantly relaxed. "Let's see, we've got the Maxwells coming to

64

dinner, haven't we? I must think about wine," he said.

*   *   *

The Trumans were nearly home. Their hunters weren't tired and they had trotted nearly the whole way. "I do hope Harriet's there," Mrs. Truman said for the seventh time. "Surely she had enough sense to turn for home when the fog came down."

"Let's hope so," Professor Truman replied. "I should imagine, knowing Harriet, that it all depends on Angela."

"What are we going to do if she isn't?" Jean asked.

"Look for her in the car, I suppose," Mrs. Truman said.

*   *   *

"Here it is," shrieked Anne, hearing a bang on the front door, running through the hall, thinking, I'm going to ride in an ambulance.

Adam felt himself break into a cold sweat. Supposing we can't find Jane, he thought, supposing she's slowly dying of exposure? It's like a nightmare, an awful endless nightmare, which is with you still in the morning and haunts you for the rest of the day.

Ursula pressed a Thermos of tea into his hands. "Take this for the girl," she said.

Two tall men in uniform stood by the front door talking to Anne. "Here you are. Let's go." one said, smiling at Adam.

He followed them to the ambulance, climbed inside and discovered that his legs felt like chewed string.

"She's in the vale, is she?" the driver asked.

"That's right," he answered. "By some rails on top of a bank."

65

"How did it happen?" the other one asked.

"I don't know," he replied. "We weren't there."

The fog was very thick in the road.

"We'll have a job to find her in this," the driver said. They crawled along at a bare ten miles an hour. Adam's hands were clammy. It will be ghastly if we look and look and still can't find her, he thought.

"What a day to go hunting on," one of the men remarked.

"It wasn't like this this morning," Anne said.

They came to some cross-roads and turned left.

"Can you remember which side of the vale the bank was on?" the driver asked.

"I don't know. I think it must have been in the middle," Adam replied, trying to remember, but seeing only Jane with her fair hair framing an ashen face, lying beneath the bank. He was very cold now without his shirt and wished he had borrowed a jersey while he was at the Mill House. And suddenly it seemed terribly important that the ambulance should hurry and he said, "Can't you go a little faster?" with a choke in his voice.

"We're doing our best, son," the driver said.

An enormous lorry drove past and then a succession of cars. And poor Angela is standing holding Trooper without a coat, Adam thought. He took off his spectacles and wiped them, he blew his nose, and still they seemed to be creeping along the same endless piece of road. Anne had disappeared into her own private world. At one point the driver got out of the ambulance to reconnoitre. We'll never be there, Adam thought, and started to bite his nails in a frenzy of impatience. They turned left again and then right, and presently the ambulance stopped and the two men started to talk together in low tones and Adam thought, they're lost.

Anne said, "What's the matter? Why don't they hurry up?"

And one of the men said, "We're just trying to work out the best way, miss."

"Isn't everything hopeless?" Anne asked, turning to Adam. "I bet you feel awful. But I don't suppose anyone could have done better than you have, and at least we've got an ambulance."

None of them heard the clip clop of hoofs as Professor and Mrs. Truman and Jean passed them like ghosts in the fog.

"Gosh, did you see, it was an ambulance?" Jean said. "I wonder where it was going."

CHAPTER SEVEN

MR. JEEVES stood outside the park blowing his horn. "They must hear that," he said turning to Major Smith. He thought, Miss Mockler will raise cain after this. What a disastrous day it is! Why can't Bill bring them out? We'll have to pay the earth if hounds kill one of her precious deer. He blew again and then he said, "I suppose we might as well ride on a bit—they may be coming out on the other side of the park."

Major Smith began another of his stories, to which Mr. Jeeves turned a deaf ear. They rode on for a time until presently they met Mrs. Pierce and Tony.

"Hallo there, have you seen my girl?" Mrs. Pierce called. And Mr. Jeeves remembered the fair girl on the thoroughbred.

"You mean the one on the big horse?" he asked. "No, I'm afraid I haven't. She looks good on a horse though. If you ever want to let her go, send her to me, I could do with her in the hunt stables, and she would probably ride second horse better than old Sam."

"I think she must have fallen off. She disappeared somewhere in the middle of the vale. I'm sure someone should look for her," Tony said.

"My dear, everyone disappeared somewhere in the vale," Mr. Jeeves said, "We can't possibly start looking for all of them."

"Some of my pupils were with her. I'm really rather worried," Mrs. Pierce said.

"I expect they'll turn up. Most people do in the end," Major Smith told her.

"What's the matter with your grey?" Mr. Jeeves asked. They rode on together for a time, and then Mrs. Pierce saw a kiosk and borrowed sixpence from Major Smith and disappeared inside. And Tony heard hoofs which she thought were probably Quickstep's, and said, "I think that's John," and disappeared down the road at a brisk trot.

"If Freemantle was any good, he would be here somewhere now," Mr. Jeeves said, thinking, what will the Hunt Committee say when they hear about the deer?

*　　*　　*

Bill was standing in the centre of the park, blowing his horn. He had collected three and a half couple of guilty-looking hounds. Somewhere not far away in the fog Bruce was vainly trying to send the rest of the pack to him, and farther away he could hear the cries of the small boy who rode a roan pony and whose name he didn't know.

He was thinking, this is probably the end, and suddenly he didn't really care any more. He was cold and the raw day seemed to have entered into the marrow of his bones. It was on these occasions that he would wonder why he had ever chosen to be a huntsman; he would envy men who worked in garages and shops and his brother who was a clerk in the offices of the Flintshire County Council. He looked at the hounds around Toby's heels, watched them avoid his eye, and said, "You rotters. Ware deer. Do you hear? Ware deer." He patted Toby. Then he put the horn to his lips and blew again and again.

Farther away, Bruce was addressing Miss Mockler.

"I'm very sorry, madam," he said. "We will have hounds out of here as soon as possible, I assure you."

In spite of the raw day there was sweat on his brow, and little brown Prudence was sweating too. He thought, why can't she leave us alone, surely she can see we're not encouraging them? He could feel his temper rising and his voice was hoarse when he added, "We want them out of here, just as much as you do."

Miss Mockler still had the branch. She waved it now.

"You'll all be prosecuted. There's a notice to that effect on the gate," she said in her high angry voice.

"Well, that'll have to wait. At the moment I have to get hounds out of here," Bruce said, riding past her, cracking his whip, crying, "Ware deer! Hold up together there," pushing Prudence into a gallop as a couple and a half of hounds rushed past close on the heels of a soft-eyed hind.

*   *   *

If only I wasn't so cold, thought Jane, trying to see how badly Trooper was hurt while she still lay covered by Angela's coat. Her head was aching and she had just been sick for the third time. She had tried to stand up, but Angela had ordered her to stay still and Jane, who felt dizzy whenever she moved her head, was quite glad to obey. What a muck I've made of everything, she thought now. I've scarred Trooper for life and most likely lost my job as well. When I'm all right I shall have to stay with Aunt Mary until I find a job, and now changing her job didn't appeal to Jane in the least. She saw herself being interviewed by prospective employers, travelling miles by train, competing against numerous other girls. And in the end taking a situation she didn't like through sheer exasperation.

Angela was rubbing Trooper with her hands, trying to keep him warm. She had stopped crying. She had reached a stage when she didn't even want to think any more, but even so her mind revolved around Adam—where was he? Why didn't he come? Or had he met with an accident? Her eyes were watering from staring hopefully into the fog and in spite of rubbing Trooper her hands were completely numb. Jane had offered her back her coat, but Angela had refused and now she was shivering. It was a long time since she had heard hounds or the horn.

Harriet had stopped crying too. She had talked a little with Jane and put her small checked riding-jacket over Trooper's large bay quarters. She had wondered how long it would be before her parents started to look for her, and had been glad that Melody and Moonlight weren't clipped like poor shivering Trooper. Once she had envied Anne and imagined her sitting snugly at home with Ursula. Now she looked at Angela and said, "I'm going to look for Adam," in a small determined voice. And Angela, suddenly too weary to argue, said, "Go if you like, but you'll never find him in this fog."

Harriet climbed nimbly over the bank, glad to be doing something at last. She untied and mounted Melody and rode away into the fog calling, "Adam, Adam, it's Harriet, where are you?"

She found a gate and opened it. She cantered on across grass. Melody, with the extra oats still inside and glad to be on the move again, gave several bucks and Harriet

70

lost a stirrup. She came to the stile which many of the field had jumped in the morning, but it was too big for Melody and she turned back. She missed the fence on the other side of the field and Melody took her back to the gate she had opened. She was exasperated by now. She rode Melody directly away from the gate and continued to call, "Adam, Adam, where art thou?"

Angela was thinking, why did I let her go? Now she will be lost too. Jane said, "Do you think anyone will ever come? Why don't we start walking?" She was feeling better. It seemed silly to wait for an ambulance if she could walk.

"Let's wait a little longer. It must come soon," Angela said.

*   *   *

"Well, you needn't have come with me if you didn't want to. Anyway here's a road," said Graham, seeing telegraph posts at last.

Lucy shook her fair curly hair and rammed her crash cap more firmly on her head. She was feeling disagreeable. The morning had been so lovely. Hearing the alarm clock, she had thought, I'm going hunting, with a sudden rush of joy. She had gobbled her breakfast before being driven by her mother to the riding school. She had enjoyed grooming Midnight and helping everyone while he was at the forge. She had felt dashing in her fawn jacket bought especially for the occasion; she had enjoyed the hack to the meet, and the sight of hounds coming into the market-place, and the exhilarating canter to the first covert, and the sound of the horn coming from among the trees and the first cry of hounds. She couldn't understand why she had ever agreed to turn for home with Graham and for the last hour she had been bitterly regretting the decision.

71

"Well, which way do you suppose we go?" Lucy asked now, staring angrily at the winding foggy road.

"I haven't a clue," Graham said. They stood and gazed one way and then another, and Lucy began to feel frightened for the first time.

"I should think it's left," Graham said at last.

"I wish we had never left Angela," Lucy said for the third time.

"Well, she may be lost too, for all we know," Graham replied.

"I wonder where Mrs. Pierce and Jane are and Adam," Lucy said, riding beside him down the road. "Do you think we'll ever find our way back?"

"Of course we will now we've reached the road. We'll stop and ask the first car which comes along," Graham replied.

"If one comes," Lucy said.

*   *   *

John thought, I shall never find her now. In the distance he could hear the horn. Alone he pursued five couple of hounds on the scent of a stag. Quickstep was tiring, twice she stumbled into a hole, and each time seemed to save herself by a miracle. Will we ever get hounds out of here? I suppose if one left them, they'd tire in the end and find their own way home, John thought. But supposing before they tired they killed a stag or one of the pretty soft-eyed hinds? It would do the hunt incalculable harm. John decided, riding outside hounds trying desperately to head them off as they hunted with cheerful cries through the bracken.

Tony was probably two-thirds of the way home by now, he thought a moment later, and saw her hacking cheerfully through the fog, her dark hair curling beneath

Then he was sliding into space

her bowler, her white tie and gold pin gleaming against the black of her coat. Why was I such a fool? Why didn't I invite her when we were riding together this morning? he asked himself and remembered that the saddest words in the English language are, *Too late*, and *If only*. But remembering that didn't make him feel any better. He thought, I'll send her a Christmas card and write on it, *Do you remember that awful day? Yours, John.*

He felt a branch grab his hat, scrape his shoulder, pull him back and back, tear his face and he thought, I'm being swept off. Why didn't I watch the trees? At one moment his head seemed to be on Quickstep's quarters and he tried to push the branch off with his hands. He felt it rip a button off his coat, then he was sliding into space; a second later he hit the ground, saw Quickstep's chestnut hocks, and the branch swing back into space, and thought, Quickstep's going and I shall never find her in this fog. Oh why was I such a fool? A second later he was alone in a bed of bracken, with the fog all around him in his nose and his eyes and his mouth, and trickling down his face was a stream of blood.

*   *   *

Professor and Mrs. Truman and Jean rode into their stableyard and with one accord they looked towards Melody's loose-box.

"She's not back," Mrs. Truman said, with a catch in her voice. "I wish we had stayed with her. Supposing she's hurt, no one will ever find her in this fog."

"It's all my fault for falling off," Jean said with a quiver in her voice.

"And where's Anne?" Professor Truman asked.

Riding along the last piece of road, they had given the usual hunting cries intended to fetch the person who had stayed at home from the house. Now suddenly they were all filled with a dreadful sense of foreboding.

"It's most odd, where can she be?" Mrs. Truman said, imagining an accident with the chaff cutter, a sudden attack of chicken pox, a bilious attack.

"We'll soon find out," Professor Truman said.

They put their horses away and then they hurried indoors. Ursula met them. "I did not hear you. I am so sorry," she said. "Anne she has gone with a boy called Adam in an ambulance to fetch a girl called Jane. Harriet is there too. They have only been gone fifteen minutes."

"That must have been the ambulance we passed on the road and we didn't know. How absurd!" cried Jean.

"It's not Harriet who is hurt, is it?" Mrs. Truman asked.

"No, Jane from the school," Ursula said.

"How frightful," Jean said.

"We'd better get out the car and see if we can find

them. It won't be easy in this fog. However on earth did the boy end up here?" Professor Truman asked.

"I expect he was lost. Adam can never find the way. Probably Sandy brought him here," Jean said.

Mrs. Truman said, "We'd better take a Thermos of coffee with us and a rug. You'd better come too, Jean. Then you can ride Melody back if Harriet's exhausted."

"What about Jane's horse? Don't you think we ought to ring up the riding school?" Jean asked.

"Yes," Mrs. Truman said, moving towards the telephone.

"I'll make the coffee," Ursula said.

Jean picked up two of the buckets arranged round the kitchen fire with sacks over them. "I'll feed the horses," she said. She was feeling desperately tired. Everything possible seemed to have gone wrong, and she was still certain that if she'd never fallen off they wouldn't have lost sight of Harriet.

The horses whinnied to her as she crossed the yard. She tipped the steaming mash into their mangers. She kissed Black Knight on the neck and said, "It wasn't your fault." She refilled their water buckets. She didn't know Jane very well. The Trumans weren't often seen at the riding school, but what she had seen she had liked, And that big thoroughbred looked awful to ride, she remembered, and Jane's not very large. Where did it happen? she wondered, switching off the stable light, walking back through the fog to the house, to the warm kitchen, which now smelt of coffee, and to Ursula hurriedly cutting sandwiches on the table.

"Hallo, is that Mr. Pierce?" Mrs. Truman asked. "I've just rung up because apparently your fair girl has met with an accident somewhere in the vale. Yes, an accident. Oh, some time ago, I think. There's an ambulance on its way to her now, but whether it will ever find her in this fog is an entirely different matter. Yes. Well, my youngest daughter is with her and a boy called Adam and Angela Clavers."

It would be someone feeble like Angela, Jean thought, why couldn't it be someone like John? He would know how to cope; he's used to bandaging up hurt animals.

"No, I'm afraid I don't know where they are," Mrs. Truman continued. "At one time they were with Angela. That's the last I saw of them, they may be still with her for all I know. Yes, a boy on a piebald and a small girl on a black. And we met your wife on our way home. She was trying to get you on the telephone. Her grey is lame. Yes, an awful day and this fog is just the end. Yes, well we're taking the car out now. Right you are. Not at all. Good-bye."

Mrs. Truman put down the receiver. "He sounds more worried about Graham and Lucy than Jane," she said.

"I'm not surprised. Their parents are probably ringing him up every five minutes," Professor Truman replied.

"I hope Jane isn't terribly hurt," Jean said.

They took the Thermos, a packet of sandwiches, a hurricane lantern, a bucket of feed, a horse rug and three blankets. They fetched their battered Ford V Eight from their garage and drove away into the fog, and Jean was thinking, will we ever find them? or will night come first? And Mrs. Truman was praying that Harriet would be all right, and Professor Truman was trying to watch the verge as they crawled along at six miles an hour.

*   *   *

Tom lit another cigarette. Bang goes my game of darts, he thought, gazing miserably into the fog from the warmth of the saddle room. Can't think what's keeping them. They can't be hunting in this, he mused. Something must have gone wrong.

Five minutes later, he looked at Fearless and saw that

he had broken out again. He turned back his rug and the yellow and red striped blanket underneath and started to rub him down with handfuls of golden straw. And it's the match on Thursday and I'll never be any good if I don't get in some practice, he thought.

CHAPTER EIGHT

EXASPERATED, Mr. Jeeves turned for home.

"I'm not going to start charging about the park. There's enough in there now," he told Major Smith. "I shall only lame poor old Dawn, and there's plenty of trouble in store for the hunt as it is."

"These single ladies can cause a deuce of a lot of trouble with their whims and fancies. I remember . . ." Major Smith began.

"I don't altogether blame poor Miss Mockler " Mr. Jeeves interrupted. "She's probably fond of her deer."

"She's a bit eccentric, though. Fancy hanging on to a big place like that. I'm told half the rooms are shut up," Major Smith replied.

"She's probably fond of the house too. Perhaps she was brought up there," Mr. Jeeves replied, remembering his own childhood in a grey house in the Cotswolds.

They left the park fence behind them at last, and when they reached Betchley the lamps were lit in the streets.

"I suppose Sam is sitting by a fire by this time, lazy beggar," Mr. Jeeves said. They parted in the market-place, Major Smith to his trailer, Mr. Jeeves to the road which would lead him home. This fog gives one claustro-phobia, Mr. Jeeves thought hacking through a silent countryside; when I get home I'd better get out the old car and see Miss Mockler before she starts suing the hunt. He felt depressed as he rode along the solitary roads. It's been the devil of a day, he thought, and this isn't the end of it, not by a long chalk.

*   *   *

Graham had managed to stop a car. He took off his crash cap and said, "I'm sorry to bother you, but please can you tell me the way to Lane End Riding School?"

"The Pierces' place," Lucy added.

The woman driving said, "I'm very sorry, we're strangers here. We're on our way to Betchley, if that's any help."

The rush of hope which had come to Graham when he first heard the car evaporated.

"It isn't really. You see I think it's this side of Betchley. We would be all right, if it wasn't for this beastly fog," Graham replied.

"You haven't a map by any chance, have you?" Lucy asked.

"No, I'm afraid we haven't. I'm so sorry, we don't seem much use, do we?" the woman said, slipping in the clutch, smiling vaguely, before driving away into the fog.

"What did I say? I knew it was hopeless," Lucy said. "Mummy and Daddy will be frantic. We'll never be allowed to hunt again. Oh, I *do* wish we had stayed with Angela." She saw her brother playing with trains on the nursery floor at home. She was the eldest of three and inclined to be bossy. Her father was the borough surveyor and adored her.

"There's no need to be so pessimistic. We may be on the right road for all we know. Anyway the fog isn't my fault, even if leaving Angela is," Graham said.

Then they heard hoofs. "Hurray," cried Lucy. "Perhaps it's Jane."

"Sounds too small for Trooper," Graham said, listening carefully.

78

"Perhaps it's Angela then," Lucy suggested, suddenly smiling and carefree again.

"More likely Adam. It's a small pony," Graham replied peering into the fog, seeing a brown pony come into sight, crying, "It's one of the Trumans."

Harriet was overjoyed when she heard voices. Riding alone backwards and forwards across the same endless fields, she had been terrified. At last in despair she had given Melody her head and very soon they had reached the road. Now with a rush of disappointment she saw that it was Lucy and Graham who stood talking together. They won't be any use, she thought, why couldn't it have been a grown-up or John or Tony?

She said, "Have you seen Adam, by any chance? He's supposed to be fetching an ambulance."

"Who for? What's happened?" Graham said.

"It's Jane," Harriet replied and suddenly she was crying again. "She came off at the bank and rails and she's been lying there for hours and hours, and she looks so awful, and Trooper's hurt too. His leg looks half off, and poor Angela is standing there without a coat, and Adam went hours ago."

"Gosh!" Graham exclaimed, and then, "How terrible."

"Poor Jane," Lucy said, trying to imagine her lying hurt beneath a bank.

"We simply must do something," Harriet said, with desperation in her voice. "Honestly she'll get pneumonia soon, and if she doesn't, Angela will."

"Well, obviously it's no good waiting for the ambulance," Graham said, suddenly becoming businesslike. "It may be bogged or completely lost, or Adam may have fallen off and never got to a telephone. We must do something off our own bat."

"Why don't we ring up for another ambulance? And then find some people with a hurdle. If we get enough help, something's sure to reach her in the end," Lucy said. "Come on, we'd better get going," she cried clattering off down the road. "First stop house with a telephone."

"That's a super idea," Graham said.

"We might as well get a doctor too," Harriet said.

*   *   *

"It's no good, I'm not going to stay here any longer," Jane said, struggling to her feet, feeling everything go round in crazy circles, keeping her balance with difficulty.

"Oh, do be careful," cried Angela. "Get hold of something."

It was then that Jane saw Trooper's wound. "But he is hurt, terribly hurt," she cried staring at the shivering bay. "Why did you say he wasn't? What are we going to do?"

She looked awful swaying beside the bank; and she didn't seem able to move one arm. What will the Pierces say? He's worth three hundred guineas, she thought. And suddenly she longed for bed and a long warm drink, and for someone to be saying, it wasn't your fault, Jane, more than anything else in the world.

"I didn't want to upset you," Angela said. And Jane asked, "Has he stopped bleeding? I wish he would stop shivering. Is he terribly lame?" Her teeth were chattering. Everything was so much worse than she had suspected, and now her head was aching, and she still couldn't remember hitting the fence or falling, or anything which had happened since the meet.

"He wasn't too bad at first. I suppose I should have kept him moving. Now he's stiff and really terribly lame. But it's a clean wound, that's one thing," Angela said, trying to sound encouraging.

"If only I could remember," Jane said.

"You must have hit your head," Angela told her.

"I suppose my hat fell off," Jane said vaguely, sitting

down on the side of the bank with her aching head in her hands.

"There's nothing much we can do then," she said presently. "I hope someone thinks of getting the trailer for poor Trooper. Do you think he'll have to be destroyed?" She thought, I shall be notorious as the girl who killed the Pierces' big bay, and his death will haunt me all my life.

"Oh, I don't think so," Angela replied in reassuring accents, though she was far from happy herself, "I've done first aid with the Guides, so I know a little about it."

Jane thought, I'm glad it's Angela who's here. Lots of people would keep talking and asking me how I felt every other minute. But she seems to understand. She said, "Wouldn't you like your coat back? I think I've had it long enough."

"If you're warm," replied Angela, who was shivering.

It was a tremendous effort for Jane to stand up, walk across to Angela and give her the coat. Her left arm seemed stiff and her shoulder felt funny.

"You look as though you've hurt your arm," Angela said with sympathy in her blue eyes. "Or do you think it's your collar bone?"

"I don't know. It's not much," Jane replied, trying to sound offhand. "Probably I'm just badly bruised."

"I think you'd better sit down again, You look awful," Angela said, and once again she thought, I wish someone would come, oh how I wish someone would come.

After a time Jane said, "This fog's a nuisance, isn't it? Do you think anyone will ever find us? I'm not worried about myself, it's Trooper I'm worried about."

She thought, I feel so helpless. If only Trooper wasn't lame we could try to find a road.

"I can't think what's happened to Adam?" Angela said, and Jane sensed despair in her voice.

"Why don't you go and let me stay here with Trooper?" she asked, getting to her feet again.

"There's no point. Harriet's already gone. We'll only end up looking for each other," Angela replied.

"I wonder where Mrs. Pierce is," Jane said after a moment. "It's funny she didn't see me come my cropper. I must have got left behind somehow."

"I think it was jolly brave of you to try this jump at all; especially on a young horse," Angela remarked, looking at the bank and smashed rail.

"I wish I hadn't now. Only when I'm riding a horse for sale, the Pierces like me to jump everything. And, of course things look smaller when you're riding a big horse like Trooper," Jane said ruefully, brushing her fair hair back off her forehead, looking at the rails, thinking, they look bigger every moment, perhaps I was a fool to try and jump them on Trooper. Will the Pierces think so? What will they say? feeling suddenly sick again.

"I feel as though we are on a desert island together," she said presently. "Often I try to decide who I would like to be marooned with; it's one of the ways I judge my friends. There's not many people one would care to share hardship with and live with for months on end."

"It's not a desert island we're on; it must be somewhere in the Hebrides or the Faroes, or off Iceland. Do I pass?" Angela asked.

"Very much so. Unfortunately, I never considered you as a candidate so it doesn't prove anything right or wrong," Jane replied.

"We're not very well equipped. We haven't even a box of matches and there aren't any fish. I think we will starve," Angela said.

"If only the fog would lift," Jane replied. "It must be after four by now."

"It'll soon be dark," Angela said with a shiver.

"I don't care about myself. It's Trooper I'm worried about," Jane said again with a choke in her voice.

"Well, if Mrs. Pierce cared, she'd be looking for you by now," Angela said.

"Probably she's on her way home with Graham and Lucy. She probably thinks I'm in front of her," Jane replied, imagining the sound of hoofs on tarmac, stable lights, warm boxes, Mr. Pierce greeting them in the yard.

"My parents will start looking for me soon," Angela said.

"I've messed up your day too, and Trooper's and Adam's," Jane said, and for a moment Angela thought she was going to cry.

"Don't be silly. I had messed up mine already. I was lost. I always am when they run across the vale," Angela said quickly.

Jane stared into the fog. Her teeth had started to chatter again and she wanted to cry. I'm a failure, she thought. I shall never be any good, and I've racked my shoulder. I knew I was doomed even before we started to the meet, I remember it now—everything went wrong; Midnight lost a shoe; I forgot my sandwiches, the Pierces were cross and so was I. Trooper wouldn't stop tossing his head and Mrs. Pierce blamed my hands and I blamed the twisted snaffle and running martingale. Probably I deserved all this; one should never be cross on a young horse, it's always fatal.

"If you lose your job, you must come and stay with us," Angela said, with a sudden rush of generosity. "I know Mummy and Daddy will love to have you. They're always telling me to invite people, and I would adore you to come."

"Thank you very much," Jane said.

*   *   *

John started to walk through the bracken calling, "Come on, Quickstep, co'up, co'up." He thought, most likely the far gates will be open and she will charge on to the main road and that will be the end of her. It's the worst day I've ever had, he decided, except for the first run with Tony, everything's gone wrong from start to finish. He mopped the blood off his face with a handkerchief, and thought of Quickstep galloping into the yard at home with stirrups flying. Thank goodness I always ride with my safety catches up, he thought and then, what will Dad say? He saw the family clustered round a sweating blowing Quickstep. They're sure to think I'm badly hurt, he decided, they might even send an ambulance and then what a fool I'd feel. If only Tony hadn't gone off on her own she might have caught Quickstep, he thought, and imagined her trotting towards him leading the chestnut, smiling and calling, "It's okay, I've caught her," but that only happens in books, in cheap romances, he thought. No one will catch Quickstep. I shall have to walk home and she may not be there when I get there. But am I going in the right direction? he thought a moment later. I don't even know that. He caught his spurs in roots and stumbled into rabbit holes. Low branches caught him by the shoulder and often the bracken was waist high. And then at last he came to what he imagined was a clearing and there was grass under his feet and a smell of pine, and he thought, this is probably the vista in front of the house. He tried to decide which way to turn, but it wasn't easy. He had never seen the house, nor been in the park before. He had only his instinct and his common sense to help him. At last he followed a well-worn path which turned left and led him through rhododendrons between pines, and then to more grass. After a time he heard hounds again and the cries of Bruce and Bill. Perhaps if I reach them they can set me on the road to home, he thought, and turned towards them and felt the blood from his face trickle on to his hunting-tie.

*   *   *

First of all the number was engaged. Then after a second attempt, Mrs. Pierce heard her husband answer. He sounded flustered and when he heard it was his wife, he said, "I've just had a call from the Trumans. Jane's had a fall. They're ordered an ambulance. Do you know anything about it?"

She said, "An accident!" and thought, oh no, how dreadful.

"They say Trooper's hurt too. They want a trailer. It sounds a proper smash up."

"Graham and Lucy aren't with her then?" Mrs. Pierce said, hoping he'd say, they're here.

"Aren't they with you? They aren't here. What a mess up. The fog's awful here. What's it like where you are?"

"Like pea soup. I rang you because Dairymaid's lame," Mrs. Pierce said.

"But what am I to do? I can't fetch both of you," Mr. Pierce replied.

"Where is Jane?" she asked.

"Somewhere in the vale. No one knows where," he answered.

"You'd better get a box for one of us. I'm on the main road. I'll keep walking slowly," she said.

She felt tired suddenly. It would be awful without Jane, and it sounded as though she really was hurt. Dairymaid kept pulling at her reins, and Mrs. Pierce had blisters on both her heels. "You'll hurry, won't you?" she said into the receiver. "Try Charlie. He must be back from market by now."

"I'll do what I can," her husband promised doubtfully. "I think I'd better fetch Trooper and send a box for you."

"I wish I knew where Graham and Lucy had got to. Is there anyone at the stables to help them if they get back before us?" Mrs. Pierce asked.

"A few kids," he answered.

They said good-bye and hung up. Mrs. Pierce stepped

85

out of the kiosk and stood gazing up the road. How long would it be before Graham and Lucy's parents started ringing up the stables? she wondered. And what about Adam? She imagined the phone ringing in the empty house. Perhaps it's a good thing Harold won't be there, she thought.

*   *   *

The hoofs Tony had heard seemed to have disappeared. She thought, it seems feeble just to hack home like this. But there really isn't much I can do. It's not as though hounds would listen to me if I joined the fray in the park. Southwind walked with a long effortless stride, obviously delighted to be on her way home. Cars crawled past them in the fog. Far away a cow mooed and nearer a dog was barking incessantly. Tony thought of Brutus welcoming her in the yard, of tea with her mother and of relaxing afterwards with a book.

"Yes, I think we're right to call it a day," she said. patting Southwind beneath her neat black plaits.

CHAPTER NINE

"THAT BOY'S a wonder," Bill said to Bruce as they counted hounds.

"He's a lot more use than Captain Freemantle," Bruce replied watching Mark ride towards them on a dripping Merrylegs.

"Well done, son," Bill called.

Mark was happy. He was doing a job, and he was one of those restless people who need to be doing a job if they're to be happy.

He smiled now and patted Merrylegs. "How many do we still want?" he asked.

"Four couple," Bill said. "And where they are I couldn't say."

"I'll look for them," Mark said, already turning Merrylegs.

"Hi, wait a minute. Have a Polo," offered Bill, who always carried peppermints with him. "It'll do your voice the world of good, and keep the cold out," he added.

Mark took one and smiled at Bill and said, "What a day!"

Bruce said, "Maybe they'll find their own way home."

"I reckon they're still hunting deer, the blighters," Bill replied. "Here, see if you can blow it, son," he added, handing Mark the horn.

Mark dismounted and let Merrylegs crop the short grass, but though he blew and blew he could make no more than a gurgling noise with the horn.

Bill was sympathetic and said, "Better luck next time," and took it back and blew *Home* until he had no breath left. After that they all ate sandwiches and Mark felt that he belonged to the hunt and started to hum John Peel.

"Suppose the Master's gone home," Bill remarked after a while.

"I don't blame him. There's not much he can do in this great park," Bruce said.

Bill lit a cigarette and presently he said, "I suppose we'd better have another try. Do you want to look for them, son?"

"Of course," Mark answered, mounting Merrylegs, riding away with Bruce, feeling about eighteen.

"Well, be careful now," Bill called after them. Five minutes later they parted. Bill was riding behind them still blowing, though there wasn't any sign of the missing hounds.

Merrylegs was tiring and Mark let her dawdle. Every few minutes he stopped to listen. And then quite suddenly he heard a neigh and the sound of a horse breaking through

Quickstep came into sight

undergrowth. Throwing her head up, Merrylegs stopped in her tracks. Mark peered into the fog. He heard the sound of hoofs on soft earth and presently Quickstep came into sight with broken reins dangling and her saddle under her stomach.

He thought, John's hunter, and was amazed because of all the Pony Club members he admired John most, and it seemed impossible that he of all people should have fallen off.

Mark dismounted and said, "Whoa little horse," and Quickstep smelt Merrylegs and let him take hold of her broken reins. He thought, there must have been some sort of accident, and then, I had better start looking for John. He put Quickstep's saddle back into place, remounted Merrylegs and rod on through the park, and now he yelled, "John, hoi John," instead of calling hounds home.

*　　*　　*

"Let's try this house. Bags ring up," Lucy cried, dismounting and throwing her reins to Graham.

I don't think she cares about Jane at all, Harriet thought disagreeably, she's simply enjoying all the excitement.

The house was low and thatched with a newly painted front door. There was crazy paving in the garden and an elm-wood garage. Harriet could see that inside the rooms were discreetly lit by electric lights in crooks and crannies. In front of the living-room fire was an array of copper kettles.

"It's very *Ye Olde*, isn't it?" she asked Graham.

"It looks as though it'll be on the telephone. I hope Lucy hurries up. I wonder if she knows the name of a doctor. I think two of us should have gone in really." Graham said:

"It might have been better," Harriet agreed.

A woman in slacks and with her hair in a pony-tail opened the door to Lucy.

"There's been an accident. Can I use your telephone? I need an ambulance," Lucy said.

The woman ushered her in. "How terrible!" she exclaimed. "How absolutely ghastly. Where did it happen?"

"In the vale," Lucy answered, hurrying to where she could see the telephone partly concealed behind some books.

"Do you know what to dial?" the woman asked.

And Lucy said, "I'm dialling 999," in a small determined voice. Outside Graham was saying, "My Ma must be in a frenzy. She didn't want me to stay out too long. I bet she's rung up the riding school half a dozen times by now."

"Poor Mr. Pierce," Harriet said.

"Poor us," Graham replied. "I'm fagged out, and I bet Ma's got a super tea waiting at home, and there was something at four I wanted to watch on TV too."

"I hate TV," replied Harriet.

"Have you ever watched it?"

"No."

"How do you know then?"

"I just know," Harriet said.

Lucy turned to the woman. "Now I want a doctor. Do you know of one?" she asked.

She felt cool and competent with the receiver in her hand. I bet our ambulance reaches Jane before Adam's, she thought.

The woman found the number of a doctor in the directory. He was called Fraser and lived only half a mile away. In no time at all Lucy was speaking to him. She told him about Jane and said that she thought the horse might need a blood transfusion, and Dr. Fraser said he would be looking for Jane in the vale as soon as he had put his coat on and got out his car, and why didn't she telephone a vet about the horse? So the woman and Lucy searched the classified directory until they found *Vets* and then they telephoned the nearest who fortunately was in, professed to know the vale like the back of his hand and promised to be with Trooper in a jiffy.

Lucy thanked the woman, offered to pay for the calls and returned to Harriet and Graham well satisfied with her work.

"I've arranged it all," she told them, taking Midnight from Graham. "There's an ambulance going from the Royal Flintshire Hospital, a doctor called Fraser, and a vet called Saunders."

"It'll be awful if they all meet with Adam's efforts," Graham said.

"They won't. Adam's probably given up and gone home," Lucy replied scornfully.

"I bet he hasn't," cried Harriet who, like all the Trumans had a soft spot for Adam, "Don't be so beastly."

"Quarrelling won't help anyone. What do we do now?" Graham asked.

"Return to the vale," Lucy replied.

*   *   *

"Here's the vale. Where now?" Professor Truman asked, stopping the car.

"Shall we try Maunder's farm. There might be someone there in the know," Mrs. Truman suggested.

"If only the fog would lift," Jean exclaimed.

"There's not much hope of that," the Professor said, starting the car again.

They crawled on again and Jean thought, shall we ever find them? If only the vale wasn't so large. We could search all night in this fog and still find nothing.

Other cars passed them. "Keep your eyes open for the ambulance," said Professor Truman.

They came at last to the farm and Mrs. Truman went inside and talked to Mrs. Maunder. She came back with her thumbs turned down. "They know nothing," she said.

"They last heard hounds at ten o'clock this morning."

"Where now?" the professor asked. They sat and thought for a time, and a stifled suffocating silence seemed to hang over everything. Then Mrs. Truman said, "Let's drive on to that farm with the pylon in the field in front of the house."

And the Professor replied, "As you like, my dear. We'd better ask at all the farms, eliminate them one by one."

Jean took a sandwich and ate it. She thought, I shall be riding Melody home by moonlight if we don't find them soon. They crawled on again brushing against the grass at the side of the road. Occasionally the fog would seem thinner for a moment and their hopes would rise, but a little farther on it would be as thick as ever, and more than once Mrs. Truman or Jean had to get out and direct Professor Truman.

They asked at three more farms and the answer was always the same, and slowly their spirits sank, and gradually dusk came softly across the vale.

*　　*　　*

Mr. Jeeves reached the hunt stables as dusk came. Tom met him as he dismounted, and took Grey Dawn.

"What sort of day did you have, sir?" he asked.

"Awful, and where Bill and Bruce are I couldn't say. Is Sam back?" Mr. Jeeves asked.

"Yes, he's just gone in for a cup of tea," Tom replied, leading Grey Dawn into her box, taking off her saddle, thinking, heaven knows when the other horses will be home.

Mr. Jeeves telephoned his wife from the saddle-room. "Darling, will you fetch me in the old car? I am at the stables. Old Sam never turned up with Minuet and the M.G.'s still in the market-place," he told her. When he had finished talking he removed his flask and sandwich case from Grey Dawn's saddle.

"They're hunting the deer in the park," he said to Tom. "Miss Mockler will have something to say; shouldn't be surprised if she took it to court."

"She's a funny old bird by all accounts," Tom said.

Presently Mrs. Jeeves drove into the yard in the old Ford, which had been Mr. Jeeves's first car. She was wearing a fur coat and her hair reached to her shoulders. Mr. Jeeves said, "Good night, Tom. I hope the horses don't keep you up too late."

He got into the Ford and said, "I think we'd better go straight to Betchley. I must try and see Miss Mockler and calm her down."

"Wouldn't you like some tea first?" his wife asked.

"There isn't time," he said.

They crawled down the drive and into the familiar road they both knew so well. "I wish we had a fog lamp on this car," Mrs. Jeeves said.

*   *   *

"Well, this looks like the vale. Which way now, son?" the driver asked, stopping the ambulance for the seventh time. But Adam didn't know. His spectacles were misty again and he had bitten his nails to the quick.

"She's somewhere right in the middle," he replied doubtfully after a pause.

"Why not get out and have a look around? You might see a landmark," suggested Anne.

He stepped out of the ambulance, but all he could see was fog, tarmac and the dim outline of a thorn hedge. "She was in the middle," he repeated, feeling useless, thinking, I'm hopeless. Why didn't I stay with Jane and let Angela get the ambulance? "We found in a wood not more than a couple of miles if that from Betchley," he added "and then I suppose we ran for about three miles before it happened."

93

"We're a long way from Betchley," the driver said to his companion. "We'd better go back."

They got back into the ambulance and turned it round, and Adam thought, they're so terribly calm, they don't seem to realise how awful Jane looked.

"Are we going back towards Betchley then?" Anne asked.

"Trying to, but in this fog we might land anywhere," the driver said.

*　　*　　*

"Come in for a cup of tea, Eileen. Goodness knows where Angela's got to," Mrs. Clavers called.

Eileen had been waiting by the stable for what seemed hours. She had thought hounds would pack up early, and anyway Angela had said, "I'll be back by four at the latest." Now she went indoors and sat on the kitchen table drinking tea with Mrs. Clavers.

"She can't be much longer," Mrs. Clavers said. "It's not like her to stay out late. She always says it isn't fair on Moonlight; you know how silly she is about being too big for him."

"Perhaps she's lost, Mrs. Clavers," Eileen suggested.

"She's generally pretty good on the way. She gets it from her father. I'm hopeless in that respect," Mrs. Clavers said.

"It'll be dark soon. It's a good thing Moonlight's grey, though it won't help much in this fog," Eileen said.

Mrs. Clavers switched on the electric light. She was beginning to feel uneasy. "Have a rock cake?" she offered, passing a plate to Eileen. "I'll give her another twenty minutes before I start ringing up people."

*　　*　　*

The telephone rang for the third time in the Pierces' house. In the yard a crowd of small children took hay to the horses which had been left behind.

"I wonder how long Mr. Pierce will be," a boy with ginger hair said.

"I hope Jane isn't hurt," said a small girl with plaits.

"I do wish Mrs. Pierce would come back," the twins remarked. Someone switched on the saddle-room light, and after a time they all drifted there and started to discuss accidents and whether a broken neck was worse than a broken back.

* * *

John stopped and listened. Far away he could hear someone calling his name. "I'm here, I'm coming," he yelled, starting to run with hope in his heart.

Mark heard an answer. He called back, "Where are you?" and pushed Merrylegs into a trot, and thought, thank goodness he isn't hurt.

* * *

Jane said, "I shall cry in a minute. Why doesn't someone come?"

"You need something to eat and a nice hot drink," Angela replied in soothing accents.

"Well, I shan't get it lying here," Jane replied, struggling to her feet, thinking, gosh, I feel awful, and it's nearly dark. I must do something. "I'm going," she said, "Unless you'd rather I stayed with Trooper and you went."

"I think it's mad for either of us to go," Angela replied. "We'll only get lost like the others."

"I shan't go far," Jane answered climbing over the bank. "I'm just going to look for the ambulance."

"Do be careful," Angela called after her.

They should have sent for a horsebox instead of an ambulance, Jane thought, walking unsteadily into the fog.

Why must she go? Angela thought, feeling horribly alone, holding shivering Trooper, wishing she hadn't forgotten her gloves.

*   *   *

In the distance Tony heard the cry of hounds. She halted Southwind and thought, they must have left the park, I wonder if John's still with them. Anxious to be home the brown pony pawed the road and snatched at her bit.

"Stand still. I can't hear a thing," Tony said. She thought, I'll wait a bit and see what happens. Maybe they're running this way. And if they are I may be able to stop them on the road. It'll soon be dark. Surely Bill's called it a day by now, she thought, and quite suddenly she felt hungry and wished she had brought some chocolate to eat on the way home.

*   *   *

Mr. Pierce drove steadily through the fog filled with a sense of foreboding. He had arranged for Charlie Trayson to collect his wife. He had put blankets in the trailer, a rug and leg bandages, antiseptic, lint and a bucket. There was a Thermos of tea in the car and a tin of biscuits and two of Jane's jerseys. Every few minutes he stopped and, stepping on to the road, listened for hoofs, and every time he turned a corner he expected to see Graham and Lucy. But though hours seemed to pass he saw nothing but the fog and an occasional car.

*   *   *

And gradually dusk, the forerunner of night, crept across the vale.

96

CHAPTER TEN

JANE DIDN'T get lost. She came to one gate and then another, and though her legs were still wobbly and her shoulder ached unbearably, she felt better. I must reach somewhere soon, she thought, and decided that while she was telephoning for a vet and horsebox for Trooper, she would beg a cup of tea.

She walked on and on, till gradually dusk turned to night, and she realised that her stomach was aching with hunger, that her head was muzzy and that quite suddenly nothing seemed to matter any more. She could see telegraph posts faint in the dark, and once she heard a car pass and she could have sworn it was only a few yards away. But without warning she was too tired to explore any farther. Her legs began to shake and her teeth to chatter.

I shall faint in a moment, she thought, sitting down on damp grass, suddenly seeing Trooper again standing with Angela by the disastrous bank. *Hopeless grief is passionless*, she remembered, thinking, I'm not going to cry. She tried to listen for a car. She meant to call, "Help, hi, stop!" when she heard one, but every few moments she would fall into uneasy sleep, and she heard nothing pass nearby. She dreamed once that she was riding Trooper; there was the bank in front again and the rails high and solid on the top. She felt him take off and then they seemed to fall through space. She wakened with clammy hands and her head seemed to be aching worse than ever. She thought, I must go on, and struggled to her feet and now she couldn't see the telegraph posts any more, and she thought, perhaps I imagined them and perhaps there isn't a road at all. Her legs were still shaky and her mouth felt dry. "I must find

D

Presently she was dreaming of Brighton again

someone," she said out loud, hoping that the sound of her voice would give her confidence.

She walked on in a kind of dream, sometimes she was at the riding school, grooming horses, lunging a young pony, teaching small children, sometimes she was a child again living with Aunt Mary in her Regency house at Brighton. She swam in the sea and rode on the Sussex Weald, and there were crumpets for tea and a blazing fire, and the bracing Brighton air in her nostrils. She reached a road at last and, feeling tarmac under her feet, came back to reality for a moment. She thought, if I turn right and keep walking I'll come to Betchley in the end. But she was too tired to walk any farther and she thought, I'll sit down and rest for a few moments and, who knows, a car may come along. So she sat down and presently she was dreaming of Brighton again and it was summer and you couldn't see the sand on the beach for people. She was quite warm in spite of the fog and she didn't notice the dark any more, nor the damp grass beneath her, nor the ambulance which passed her presently with Adam and Anne inside. She ran happily along the Brighton sand dodging the people and presently she slept.

*   *   *

John could see that it was the little boy with freckles who had caught Quickstep. He called, "Thanks a lot. I thought I would never see her again."

"That's all right. I hope she hasn't damaged her saddle," Mark said. He was glad he had found John at last. Now he could return to helping Bill and Bruce.

"They're still hunting deer, you know," he said next. "Isn't it awful? I met the woman who owns the park and she was furious." Then he saw John's face. "But you're hurt," he cried.

"Oh, it's nothing. I got swept off by a branch," John replied, brushing his face with his hand and feeling it come away sticky.

"It looks awful. Can't we do anything?" Mark asked, peering at him in the gathering darkness. It looks filthy, he thought, it may go septic or he'll get tetanus, anything may happen.

"They'll see to it when I get home," John replied, thinking, when I get home, seeing his mother and father peering anxiously into the darkness, the light in the cowsheds, the cracked tea-pot waiting for him on the stove. "I think we both ought to start for home," he said. "I expect your mother's wondering where you are, and I'm sure mine is worried about me."

"I'm going to help get the rest of the hounds first," Mark replied. "Do you mind if I push on now?"

"I'll help you," John said, taking Quickstep, untwisting

her stirrups, mounting, realising that he was stiff all over. But Mark had already disappeared and quite suddenly darkness seemed to descend and John thought, shall I ever get out of here? and his face started to ache, and he realised that he was desperately tired and that he felt as though he had been beaten all over with a stick.

I'm sure that small boy should go home, he thought, and wished that he could remember his name, and listened for the cry of hounds, but heard nothing but his own breathing, the beat of Quickstep's heart and the rustle of trees. I'd best try to find the road, he thought, and he pushed Quickstep gently with his legs, and they moved on through the eerie and suddenly deserted park.

*　　　*　　　*

I don't believe we'll ever find her, Adam thought, and now the ambulance had stopped again and someone was opening a gate and Adam could see the outline of fir trees, and Anne was saying, "Is this the wood, Adam?"

He tried to remember the morning, the meet, the hack to the covert, the moment when the first hound spoke. He smelt the air. If only it was light.

"Well?" the driver inquired, and Adam realised with dismay that he was being addressed.

"I think so. It looks like it," he said.

They drove on, bumping over rough ground. Another gate was open, cows moved out of their way, a dog barked. It was very dark and the fog seemed even thicker in the fields. "There's a wire fence. I'll see if I can find a gate," one of the men said.

"Would you like me to look?" Adam offered, but the man was already running about in the dark. They turned round eventually and drove back across grass. And Anne said, "What hours seem to have passed since we ran into one another, Adam."

"Yes," he replied. "Hours and hours." But it's still longer since I left Angela and Jane, he thought and suddenly felt hopeless, and assailed by a great despair.

"We'll reach her in the end," the driver said.

They came to another gate and then they were bumping over plough, and Adam said, "We never came this way. All the fields we crossed were grass."

But the driver only replied, "Well, maybe we'll reach them this way, son," and he caught Anne looking at him with large mournful eyes. If only it was all a dream, he thought, but it isn't, it's all unbearably real, and he thought if only it was all over and another day, but will it ever end? Will we ever find her?

He opened another gate. It was old and cracked and sagged at the hinges; he shut it with difficulty and clambered into the ambulance again through the back doors, and sat beside Anne. A faint light glowed above them, they could see very little outside through the darkened windows, and then quite suddenly they heard someone talking, and suddenly hope came back to Adam, and the driver stopped the ambulance and they all jumped out on to the grass and Anne cried, "Hallo, there," and one of the men called, "Anyone around?" Adam could feel his heart thumping wildly.

"Oh, I hope it's them," Anne cried.

And then they heard someone call, "I'm over here," and Adam said, "It sounds like Angela," and started to run through the fog and the dark, crying, "We've brought an ambulance. Are you all right?"

*   *   *

"Well, I'm going to call it a day," Bill said to Bruce and Mark, "the other hounds can find their own way home. We can't do much anyway." He blew *home* for the last time and sadly it echoed through the silent park.

He turned his chestnut Toby and rode to where he knew the drive was, and thought, I wonder if the Master's back. The horses were tired, they stumbled into holes and against trees, they showed little enthusiasm when the road was reached eventually and their heads were turned for home.

Only little Welsh Merrylegs had energy left and Mark marvelled as he watched her gay roan ears, and felt her quick short stride cover the ground with startling rapidity. He remembered now that his mother had told him not to be late. What was she thinking now? he wondered, and hoped that she wasn't watching for him in the road. Except for that he was completely happy. He felt that he and Merrylegs had done great work which was the more amazing considering the way in which the morning had started. Bill and Bruce couldn't praise Merrylegs enough.

"I would back her to last out any of the big horses," Bill had said.

And Bruce had exclaimed, "If only a few hands bigger what a hunter she would make."

"No thank you. She wouldn't be mine if she was," Mark had replied, and had wondered what life would be like without Merrylegs.

Now he was humming "You are my sunshine," and hoping that his father had thought of putting hay and a feed in the field. He hoped too that tea would be still waiting for him on the well-worn kitchen table. His mouth watered when he thought of the sticky lardy-cake which should be there and the mountains of bread and jam. And what a lot I shall have to tell them, he thought next, and saw himself relating the day's events over a steaming cup of tea.

Hounds made little noise as they padded along the road, and the horses' hoofs seemed muffled by the fog and the dark. Bill and Bruce rode side by side smoking and talking. The night grew darker. Somewhere above their heads an owl hooted.

*　　　*　　　*

Mr. Jeeves stopped his car outside the house in Betchley Park. He adjusted his hunting-tie and stepped on to the gravel drive. He felt in his pocket for a cigarette and then decided not to smoke. Feeling like a small boy again he banged the massive door knocker and waited uneasily.

Miss Mockler opened the door to him herself, saw his scarlet coat, stiffened visibly and said:

"What do you want?"

"To apologise," he replied. "May I come in?"

She led him to a drawing-room over-crowded with furniture.

"I suppose you're the Master," she said.

*　　　*　　　*

"Are you sure this is the vale?" Graham asked.

"Of course it is. I'm not an idiot," Lucy replied.

Harriet thought, why must she be disagreeable? Then saying, "Melody's tired," she dismounted and walked along the rutted track which Lucy insisted was part of the vale.

Presently Graham said, "I shall have to start for home soon. My Ma will be having kittens. She doesn't like me being out after dark."

"I'm sure Mummy's having five hundred and fifty fits. Why didn't we think of ringing them up?" Lucy asked.

"Because we're imbeciles. Goodness knows what my parents are doing," Harriet replied.

The track seemed endless. "I don't believe this is in the vale at all," Graham said after a time.

There were high hedges now on each side of them, boughs hung overhead. It was very dark.

"Well, what do you want us to do?" Lucy asked.

"I don't know," Graham said.

They halted and Harriet said, "We really are lost now, aren't we?" and gave a little shiver.

"I've never been along here before, I know that," Graham told them.

My legs are aching, I'm tired and I feel terribly hungry, Harriet thought. And now quite suddenly she longed for home with all her being. Why did all this have to happen to me? she wondered. I was enjoying myself so much until we found Jane.

"We'd better turn back. At least we can ask people if we are on the road," Graham said.

So they turned round and led their tired ponies along the rutted lane, and Harriet wondered whether her parents and Jean were home yet and what Anne was doing. And Graham thought about tea again, and Lucy decided that she would cry soon if they did not find someone to direct them on to the right road. They stumbled over ruts and Graham suddenly exclaimed, "If this is hunting, I'd rather stay at home, thank you."

"Don't be silly, it's not always like this," Harriet replied, "sometimes it's heaven," and she remembered past hunts which had ended happily with a bran mash for Melody and tea and a hot bath for herself.

*　　*　　*

The Trumans had reached the vale. They drove carefully, but all the same, quite soon, the car was stuck in a gateway. It was very muddy and when Jean stepped out she felt mud against her ankles. Professor Truman called, "I'll try without you two on board," and revved up the engine, but still only the wheels whizzed round making a sort of purring noise in the mud.

"We'll push," cried Mrs. Truman, who was standing

beside Jean. Professor Truman revved up the engine again and Mrs. Truman and Jean pushed, but still with no avail. "We'll have to get some branches," Mrs. Truman said.

There were no trees nearby, and it wasn't easy to find branches, but eventually they collected a few and tried again, but still the car wouldn't move.

"This is a ghastly day!" exclaimed Mrs. Truman. They collected more branches to thrust under the wheels and all pushed and quite suddenly the car moved.

Jean cried, "Hurray," and slammed the gate and they drove on across the vale, until presently they saw lights shining through the fog; and Professor Truman said, "It looks like a car."

"Or an ambulance," Jean cried.

"A sign of life anyway," Mrs. Truman said. And suddenly they became excited and Jean cried, "Drive faster, Daddy," and Mrs. Truman said, "I remember crossing this field now. We turned back at the bank. Do you remember, Charles?" And they were filled with hope as they drove on towards the lights shining so dimly in the fog.

*　　*　　*

Angela thought, if Jane goes mad it will be all my fault. Why didn't I stop her going? She had always hated the dark, now she disliked it even more than usual. She had taken off her coat and put it over Trooper, so that he had two coats, hers and Harriet's. She had tried to persuade him to walk a little. She had said, "Come on, just one step. You never know, if you walked a little you might loosen up."

But the big thoroughbred was not to be persuaded. He stood with drooping head, sad ears, shivering and resting his damaged leg. Angela couldn't bear to look at him any more. And on the other side of the bank stood dear, patient uncomplaining Moonlight. Angela called to him at intervals, and once he answered with a low whinny. In spite of the two horses, she felt terribly alone, and she couldn't help thinking of her parents and Eileen waiting for her at home. And then quite suddenly she heard an engine and she said, to Trooper, "I believe someone's coming at last," and then she thought, but supposing it's the ambulance? Jane's gone. They'll be furious. Oh, why did I let her go? and she prayed that it would be a horsebox which came at last towards her through the fog. Her mouth felt dry. She called, "I'm over here," and someone cried, "We've brought an ambulance. Are you all right?" and she thought how shall I tell them that Jane has gone?

CHAPTER ELEVEN

THE CRY of hounds seemed very near now. I must watch out for traffic and try to stop them at the same time. It won't be easy, Tony thought, wishing that John was with her. She tried cracking her whip without success, and then she heard a rustling noise and Southwind snorted, and she saw a fox slither down the bank on to the road and disappear. I know where hounds will come out now, she thought, with fast beating heart, and heard a car approach and watched it pass like a ghost in the fog. I bet Mummy's anxious and Daddy's probably back by now, she thought, and then she saw the first hound, and cried, "Stop!" and, "get back with you," and at the same moment she heard a car approaching and there didn't seem any time left. More hounds were pouring into the road and she called. "Ware hounds," and the car stopped and she felt like cheering. Two couple of hounds had stopped and stood looking at her with guilty expressions. She yelled, "Thank you," to the car driver

and said, "Good hounds," and thought how ineffectual
it sounded. What should I say to them? she wondered
as the car disappeared.

She wished that she had attended to Bruce more now,
and wondered how she would ever get her two couple
of hounds back to kennels. Already they were beginning
to look sly as though they knew she didn't understand
them. She said, "Come along, we're going home," and
Southwind understood and started to walk away along
the road. And then Tony heard another hound hunting
alone somewhere behind her. She turned Southwind,
saw a car approaching, thought, they'll meet, cried, "Stop!"
heard a screech of brakes, and then a lorry swept past
her and she discovered that her heart was pounding and
that she had broken into a sweat. Farther back, she saw
something move in the darkness and then lie still. With a
knot in her throat she rode back; already she knew what
she would see, and she was overwhelmed with a sense of
failure, if only I had been quicker, if only I had been
listening, she thought.

She dismounted and looked at the big dog hound lying
in the centre of the road. He was quite dead and silently
she began to cry and her tears fell on the tarmac and ran
down her face in rivulets.

*   *   *

Mrs. Pierce waved her arms when she saw the horsebox
approaching. She thought, at last, and then, I wonder
if Harold's reached Jane yet.

The driver of the box leaned out and called, "Mrs.
Pierce?" and she shouted back, "Hallo, Charlie."

"What a night," he said stopping the horsebox. "What's
the trouble? Horse lame?"

"Yes, he slipped off at a gate," Mrs. Pierce explained.
"I seem to have been walking for hours."

107

He was quite dead

"I'm sorry I couldn't get to you earlier. But you know how it is on market day," Charlie said.

He wore a cap, a hacking-jacket, darned trousers and working boots. He let down the ramp and said, "There's a haynet inside."

Together they settled the big grey in the box. "It's a rotten night for driving," Charlie said.

"Or for anything else," Mrs. Pierce replied, climbing into the cab, thinking, home at last.

"I'm afraid I shall have to take my time. Can't see a thing in this fog," Charlie said.

*   *   *

John reached a road eventually and Quickstep knew which way to turn. Now that her head was turned to home, she seemed tireless. She settled into a hound jog and John sat in the saddle with his mind miles away. After a time he saw lights coming to meet him and he guided Quickstep into the side of the road and saw that it was an ambulance and thought, "Some poor wretch must be going to hospital."

The driver leaned out and called, "Can you tell us if we're near the vale?"

And John replied, "It's the other side of the park. Which farm do you want?"

"We don't want a farm. There's been a hunting accident," the driver said, and John's heart leapt and his first thought was Tony! But it can't be her, he decided, because she wouldn't be in the vale.

"Do you know who it is?" he asked, and the man shook his head and replied, "Couldn't say. We only know that there's a girl lying by a bank just about in the middle of the vale. How we're expected to find her in this fog, I don't know."

"Can I be any help? I know the vale pretty well," John

109

offered. "And I jumped the bank and rails this morning.

"I'm afraid you'd hold us up. It would be all right if you hadn't a horse. Can you give us directions?"

So John directed them and then he rode on deep in thought. He decided after a time that it must be Jane and wondered why the ambulance had been summoned at such a late hour. She must be terribly cold, if she had been lying there since midday, he thought, and he wished now that he could have left Quickstep somewhere and gone in the ambulance with the two men. He remembered Trooper now and how beautifully Jane had controlled him outside the first covert, he was a big bay thoroughbred, he remembered, and wore a twisted snaffle and martingale. How long ago it all seems, he thought and yet it was only this morning.

A big lorry passed him and then a car. He was glad that he was on the main road; at least there was plenty of room. He turned a corner and suddenly there was a horse in front of him, and a tall figure, which could only be Tony, bending over something. Nearby were two couple of dejected hounds watching her with guilty faces and drooping sterns.

"Tony," he cried, "what's happened?" and then he saw that she was bending over a hound and that the hound was dead. He saw too that she was crying, and was suddenly touched, because she wasn't the sort of girl you expected to cry.

She said, "Hello, John," and she sounded tired. She thought, thank goodness someone's come. I couldn't have borne to ride home alone, not after this.

He gave her his handkerchief and said, "It's Thunder. Don't cry. It's not as though he's a young hound. He's had his day."

"It's still awful," she cried, "and I could have stopped it happening, if only I had heard the car."

"There's always *if only*, life is studded with *if onlys*. After all you saved the rest, didn't you?"

Tony told him what had happened, and when she had finished, he said, "Gosh, it certainly isn't your fault. How were you to know that Thunder was going to come out like that all on his own?"

"I ought to have been listening," she replied.

"But even then you wouldn't have been in time. You were too far down the road," he said.

He picked up poor dead Thunder and put him on the verge beside the road. And Tony began to cry again and said, "It's been such an awful day."

John spoke to the hounds and presently they began to wave their sterns and to smile at him.

"You are marvellous. They wouldn't even look at me," Tony said.

After a time Tony and John rode on together with hounds at their horses' heels. And quite suddenly they seemed to have become friends.

John heard himself inviting Tony to tea and heard her gay laugh when she replied, "How funny. I was going to ask you." And suddenly he was completely happy. *All's well that ends well*, he thought. And *it's an ill wind which blows nobody good*.

But Tony was still remembering Thunder and presently they were riding side by side in that silence which can be more companionable than speech.

Later John told Tony about Jane and her face clouded again, and she said, "I thought that horse looked awful to ride. Poor Jane!"

They discussed Jane after that and the road grew darker, and except for their voices, the pad of hounds, and the sound of hoofs on tarmac, there was no noise.

*　　*　　*

111

"We're here at last," cried Adam, and then as he started to climb the bank, "where's Jane?"

"Gone," cried Angela, and her voice sounded hoarse and exhausted. "She wouldn't stay here any longer. She went off into the fog."

All for nothing, Adam thought, and Anne said, "What's the matter? Where is she?"

"Gone," Adam answered, sitting down on the bank, suddenly tired.

"Gone?" Anne echoed. "But where? I thought she was hurt."

"She is—she was," Angela replied. "It'll probably kill her wandering about in the fog. But she wouldn't wait any longer and I couldn't go with her, because of Trooper."

Anne looked at the bay. "He has hurt himself, hasn't he?" she said.

"Where's the young lady?" the ambulance men asked.

"Gone," replied Adam.

"I'm terribly sorry," Angela said, starting to apologise. "We waited for ages and ages, and she got so cold, and goodness knows where she is now."

"Her back can't be broken then," the driver said, and he sounded faintly disagreeable.

"Here, have this. You look cold without a coat," the other man said, climbing over the bank and handing Angela a blanket, but she put it over Trooper and he said, "I'll fetch you another for the horse."

"What a rum do," the driver said, and lit a cigarette.

"Has she been gone a long time?" he asked presently, and Angela replied, "About three-quarters of an hour I should think."

Normally she hated letting people down, now quite suddenly she didn't care any more. She thought, they can take over now, my part's finished.

"Did she hit her head? Do you think she was concussed?"

112

"Yes, definitely. She couldn't remember anything and that's one of the signs, isn't it?" Angela replied.

"Sounds as though we'd better look for her," he said. He's really quite nice, Angela thought. It can't be pleasant to be dragged miles only to find that your case has disappeared.

"Has anyone done anything about a box for Trooper?" she asked and then suddenly she saw lights shining through the fog and cried, "There's a car coming."

But it wasn't a car which drew up alongside the bank, but an ambulance, and suddenly Angela felt sick, and Adam thought, I must be going mad. And Anne cried, "It's another ambulance. What *has* happened?"

Two men stepped out of it looking remarkably like the other two men and said, "Where is the casualty?"

Then they saw the other ambulance and one of them said, "I see we've been forestalled."

Adam, suddenly on the defensive, cried, "I didn't order two." And Angela began to giggle. The men stared at each other.

"But where's Harriet?" Anne cried, suddenly remembering her sister. "You said she was here too."

"She disappeared a couple of hours ago," Angela replied, suddenly serious again. "I should think she's home by now."

The ambulance men exchanged cigarettes. And Angela said, "I do feel awful. I wish someone had thought of ordering a box for Trooper. I'm sure he's going to have pneumonia."

Adam said, "I'm sorry, I don't seem much use, do I?" with a choke in his voice.

"I should have thought of it. I can't think why I didn't," Angela replied.

"I hope Harriet is home by now, or Mummy and Daddy really will be flapping," Anne said.

"How am I to get home?" asked Adam, suddenly

113

imagining his parents anxiously telephoning the riding school.

"We must think of Trooper first. You'll have to travel in one of the ambulances and telephone the Pierces as soon as you can, then they'll send the trailer."

"Blimey, what's this now?" exlaimed one of the men and Anglea turned and saw lights coming through the fog. It simply can't be another ambulance, she thought.

* * *

"I hope the other hounds find their way home," Bill said. "Old Thunder's one that's missing."

They were nearly home. They had proceeded steadily at a hound jog for the last couple of miles, now Bill let Toby walk, and Bruce said, "It won't be funny if they're still in the park to-morrow morning."

"They'd left the park. I'm certain of that," Bill replied.

Soon I shall leave them, Mark thought, and my wonderful dream will be over. When I'm older I shall become a whip like Bruce, he decided suddenly, seeing himself gown up in scarlet coat, white tie, white breeches, mahogany-topped boots, spurs. I shall ride a horse like Prudence, or Toby, but whatever happens I shall always love Merrylegs best.

* * *

Mrs. Clavers was telephoning the riding school. Mrs. Pierce answered. "Yes, I know where she is, she's with my girl, Jane, who's met with an accident."

"Well, please tell her to come home right away. I'm very sorry about your girl, but really Angela mustn't stay out any longer," Mrs. Clavers replied.

"I'm afraid I can't. You see I don't know exactly where Jane is," Mrs. Pierce said. "My husband is looking for her now."

114

"I see," said Mrs. Clavers. "Is there any point in our joining the search, do you think?"

"That's up to you, Mrs. Clavers," Mrs. Pierce answered. "She's somewhere in the middle of the vale. The Trumans rang up my husband, apparently their little girl's there too."

What an unholy muddle! thought Mrs. Clavers. All the same she was relieved; at least it wasn't Angela who had met with the accident.

Presently she rang off, and looking round her pleasant chintzy drawing-room, she thought, I will wait till Guy gets home, perhaps he'll have an idea.

*   *   *

Mrs. Pierce returned to the stables and Adam's, Lucy's and Graham's parents telephoned in vain.

Mark's mother cleared away the tea things. Mrs. Simons said, "What can have happened to John? It's nearly six and it isn't like him to be late."

"Maybe they've had the run of the season, you never know. Don't worry, Mother," said broad-shouldered, kind, bluff Mr. Simons.

"You'd better clear the table," Mrs. Selwyn Jones told the parlourmaid. "I simply can't imagine where Tony's got to."

"I hope she hasn't met with an accident," the maid replied.

*   *   *

"We must be nearly there," cried Jean.

"It's like searching in a haystack," exclaimed Professor Truman.

"I should think we've covered most of the vale by now," said Mrs. Truman.

* * *

Still dreaming of Brighton, Jane slept uneasily by the roadside, a muddled sleep of exhaustion and shock.

CHAPTER TWELVE

AN AUSTIN saloon drew up beside the two ambulances and out of it stepped a tall man in a grey suit.

"Who can this be?" thought Angela.

Perhaps it's Jane's father, thought Adam, and then remembered she hadn't one.

"You seem to have got plenty of ambulances," the man said with a smile. "Where's the casualty?"

Angela felt her heart sink. Whoever he was, he expected like the others to see Jane.

The ambulance men were talking together.

"She's gone," Adam said, looking at the ground.

"The casualty he means," added Anne.

"How did you know about it?" Angela asked.

"I'm terribly sorry. Are you her father?" asked Anne, who didn't know Jane's parents were dead.

The man looked at them all as though they were a little mad. Angela felt like giggling again. It's only nerves, she thought, putting her fist in her mouth.

"It's really most annoying. I'm a busy person," the man said. "I've wasted an hour getting here, and now you say the girl's gone."

"But if you're not Jane's father, how do you know about her?" Anne asked.

"I'm Doctor Fraser. I received a message to come here as soon as possible to look at a girl with a suspected broken back. All I can say is her back can't be very bad if she can get up and walk away," he said.

"It's my fault about the back. I thought at first it was broken, but I still can't see who rang you up," replied Angela.

"Sounds like my sister," Anne said.

"You mean Harriet?" asked Adam.

The men were starting up their ambulances. They called, "Good night, Doctor," and the driver of the first one said, "We'll keep looking for her, we can't leave her out in a night like this."

They disappeared into the fog and the dark and the doctor said, "Well, I suppose I'd better be pushing off too," and suddenly he began to laugh, and Anne saw that he was quite young with a mop of fair hair and blue eyes, and Angela thought, he's rather a dear. Adam said, "I'm sorry we brought you all this way for nothing, sir."

"Well, I suppose no one can help it if the casualty gets up and walks," the doctor replied. "But where do you think she is now? If she's had a nasty spill, wandering about in this fog won't do her any good."

"I wish I knew," Angela said.

"So do I," Doctor Fraser replied.

Trooper had stopped shivering. Angela had put both blankets over him and he looked funny and rather pathetic peeping out of them.

Doctor Fraser said, "I'll look at the horse anyway."

Anne whispered to Adam, "Isn't this all rather awful? Why on earth did Jane have to go away, and I wish I knew where Harriet had got to."

Dr. Fraser untwisted the hunting-tie wound round Trooper's forearm with gentle hands. "It is in a mess, isn't it?" he asked. He fetched a bag from the car, and

He dressed the wound

as he dressed the wound, Trooper stood with soft eyes, nuzzling his back.

"I should think this will put him out of action for a long time," Doctor Fraser said when he had finished patting Trooper. "He looks a nice horse too."

"Do you ride?" asked Anne

"I used to, but I don't get much time now," he said. "Well, I'd better be going. Is there any more I can do for you? I'll keep an eye out for the casualty. But with any luck someone will have picked her up by now."

Angela looked at Anne before she said, "Can you possibly get a horsebox sent, please?"

"Of course. Anyone in particular?" Doctor Fraser asked.

"He'd better ring the riding school, hadn't he?" Adam asked.

Angela told him the number. They watched him go, and Anne said, "I suppose we ought to have cadged a lift," and Adam replied, "We can travel back in the trailer."

Everything seemed very quiet without the ambulances and Doctor Fraser. Adam started to relate to Angela exactly what had happened, and then they saw more lights approaching through the fog, and Angela cried, "Not another ambulance!"

And Anne said, "If only it could be a horsebox for a change."

Adam started to bite his nails again, and now they could see it was a car, and Angela cried, "Whoever can it be?"

*   *   *

Mr. Jeeves said, "I'm so glad you see my point," and shook hands with Miss Mockler. Secretly he was delighted with their interview. After an hour's discussion on nearly every subject under the sun, he knew he had won her round.

"And remember tea with my wife on Tuesday," he

reminded her. Thinking, Chris will be furious, he ran lightly down the steps to his car, a dashing slim figure in scarlet. He thought, my next disagreeable task will be getting rid of Freemantle, but I shall leave that to the hunt committee. He started to think about the coming meet as he drove carefully down the drive. He would have to see John's father, maybe he would offer to have a meet at their farm. Then he fell to thinking about Jane; somehow he meant to employ her in the hunt stables, he was tired of old Sam losing hounds after the first covert and going home. He can stay as stud groom, but I need young blood for my second horseman, he thought, and Tom hasn't the nerve to hunt a yard. No, it will have to be that fair girl, he decided, by hook or by crook. He was accustomed to getting what he wanted and already he saw Jane in his mind's eye working among the hunt horses. I'll see if Bruce and Bill are home yet, he decided, turning down a narrow lane which would take him to the kennels.

*　　　*　　　*

John and Tony reach Betchley.

"We'll have to go to the kennels," John said. "It's a bit out of our way to say the least, but I think we ought to deliver these hounds, don't you?"

"You make them sound like fish. But what have you done to your face?" she cried, seeing it suddenly by the light of a street lamp.

"Oh, just scratched it," John replied.

"You've done more than that. Stop a minute and let's look.

"It's certainly more than a scratch," Tony continued after a moment. "And it's filthy and will probably need a stitch. Why didn't you say something about it? Doesn't it ache?"

"Well, it does a bit. Mum will deal with it when I reach home," John said.

"You are a donkey, honestly—not saying a thing about it," she said.

Hounds stayed close to them as they rode through the town. There was little traffic about. The shops were shut. Only a few men returning from work bicycled along the streets. The church clock told them it was five past six.

"I hope you like my mother. She's a wonderful person really," he said.

"I'm sure I will," she replied.

He thought of her eating tea with them, and imagined himself showing her round the farm. "This is our accredited herd," he would say and show her the cows one by one. After that there would be the pigs to see, and the rolling acres which his father owned, and the spinney and the little copse on the hill.

She thought, I shall wear my corduroy trousers. They're the most suitable thing I've got for a farm in winter and she saw herself leaning on a gate with John admiring the view and discussing which day would suit him to come to tea at the Manor.

He thought, I'm sure Mum and Dad will like her and glanced at her turned up nose, her level forehead and her brown eyes.

Tony thought, probably Mummy wouldn't like him much, but I don't care. At sixteen, I'm old enough to choose my own friends and I think Daddy will even if Mummy doesn't.

They had left Betchley behind now, and, as they turned away from their homes towards the kennels, both horses slackened their pace.

In spite of everything, this has really been a lovely day, Tony decided, though I'm sorry about poor Thunder.

At that moment, John thought, it can't be true! "There's someone walking just in front of us," he cried, staring into

121

the dark. "I can hear the tread of hunting-boots. I think it's Jane."

*　　*　　*

"There they are," yelled Jean, leaping out of the car. "I knew we'd find them in the end. Harriet, where are you? Are you all right?" She felt quite hysterical now they had found them at last.

"Gosh, it's the Trumans," cried Angela, thinking, Harriet isn't here. How ghastly everything is.

"Hallo," shrieked Anne. "Harriet's gone, but I'm still here."

"Oh no, you don't mean to say we still haven't found Harriet," Mrs. Truman said.

"We think she's probably home by now," Anne replied. "She's been gone for at least two hours."

"I'm so sorry, Mrs. Truman," Angela said.

"It's not your fault. You're not Harriet's keeper," Professor Truman replied.

Anne started to tell them about the two ambulances and Doctor Fraser. "But *where* is Jane. You don't mean to say she's gone too," exclaimed Mrs. Truman.

Angela took up the story then. "But how terrible," cried Mrs. Truman when she had finished. "Here, have some coffee and a jersey," said Professor Truman, fetching a pile of things from the car. He handed round sandwiches and gave Trooper the feed they had brought, and replaced the blankets with a proper horse rug. "You look frozen," he told Angela.

"I'm all right, thank you," she replied, and felt two large tears trickle down her cheeks. What's the matter with me, there's nothing to cry about now, she thought.

"I think you've been marvellous, staying with Trooper all this time by yourself," Mrs. Truman said.

"A little way back we saw some lights over here," the professor said.

"It must have been the doctor's car. He hasn't been gone long," Anne told him.

Watching Trooper eating his feed, feeling the hot coffee trickle down her throat, Angela began to feel better. Perhaps everything will be all right now, she thought, perhaps Harriet really is back at the Mill House and Jane being picked up by one of the ambulances, or already in hospital.

Jean said, "I think Angela's pony should have some of the feed," and took two double handfuls away from Trooper and gave them to Moonlight.

Adam thought, it's really all over now, and saw the dim hall in the rectory, and tea waiting for him in the dining-room, which had oak furniture and beige wallpaper. Sandy will have to stay where he is, he decided, unless Mr. Pierce likes to fetch him in the trailer.

They finished the coffee and the sandwiches and then they saw another car approaching and Angela cried, "Not another ambulance!"

And Mrs. Truman said, "Who can it be this time?"

The car, which stopped alongside them, was a large and battered Standard. Out of it stepped a man wearing a cloth cap, checked jacket, gaiters and boots, who, they all knew at once, was a vet.

He didn't say, "Where's the casualty?" But looked at Moonlight and said, "Where's he hurt?"

"It's the horse over here," Anne and Angela called from the other side of the bank.

"It's one of the Pierces' horses, a big thoroughbred," Mrs. Truman told him.

He clambered over the bank, muttering, "Nasty place."

"Who can have sent him? I don't know him at all," said Mrs. Truman.

He had an enormous torch. He looked at Trooper and said, "He's been bandaged up very beautifully, who's responsible?"

Angela told him about Doctor Fraser, while he undid the bandages and examined the wound. "That's all right for the time being," he said, doing them up again. "I'll just fetch my bag from the car and give him an anti-tet' injection."

"He's nice, isn't he?" Angela asked Adam.

And then they saw another car coming and Anne cried, "It's got a trailer behind," and suddenly they all began to cheer.

"What's happened?" the vet asked, looking bewildered, and Anne cried, "It's the trailer for Trooper," and started to jump up and down.

*　　*　　*

They had reached a road. Harriet was discussing pony books with Graham. Lucy was feeling left out and had decided to sulk. Then they saw an old man on a bicycle whom they stopped and asked the way to Betchley and he told them that they were on the right road.

"At long last," cried Harriet. "If only the shops were open we could buy chocolate. I've got sixpence."

"I should think everything must have reached Jane by now," said Lucy happily, forgetting her sulks. "Poor Adam, I wonder what's happened to him?"

"I'm not going to start looking for anyone else," replied Graham. "He can find his own way home."

They came at last to Betchley, to the lights, dim in the fog, and the shops shuttered.

"I know the way from here," Harriet said, thinking, in spite of everything, to-day's been fun, at least we've lived.

"I shall be jolly glad to get home," Graham said, "and I shall think twice before I hunt again."

Lucy was silent, thinking with satisfaction of the ambulance she had ordered conveying Jane to hospital, the doctor having fixed her back in splints, the vet treated Trooper. She thought, perhaps she'll write and thank me when she knows it was me who organised everything. She ought to be jolly grateful. She saw herself telling her mother and brothers about her efficiency, in the modern nursery at home, which was distempered cream and had linoleum on the floor, and one solitary picture of poplar trees.

And then Harriet cried, "It's funny, but I can hear people talking in front, and hoofs. Can you?" and she urged Melody into a trot and clattered away down the road.

"Hi, wait," cried Lucy, who liked to be first on a scene.

"What's happened now? I'm not stopping again. I want my tea," said Graham.

*   *   *

Mrs. Pierce answered the telephone. It was Lucy's mother. She was very angry. "It's dark and there's a fog, and you say she isn't back yet," she said.

"I'm very sorry indeed for what has happened," Mrs. Pierce apologised. "My girl, who was in charge of the children, met with an accident. It's one of those things which just can't be helped."

"Well, what are you doing about it?" demanded Lucy's mother.

It was a long time before Mrs. Pierce managed to mollify Lucy's mother; and directly she had replaced the receiver Mrs. Clarke rang up and wanted to know where Adam was. She was completely exhausted by the time she had finished talking to Mrs. Clarke, and the worst of it was there was simply nothing she could do; there was only the one car, and Mr. Pierce was looking for Jane with that and the trailer. There was no point in walking along the road hoping to meet the children; most likely they had been lost and were now on their way home, she thought, but there was always

125

the chance that one of them might have met with an accident. Feeling very worried, Mrs. Pierce poured herself out a cup of tea.

CHAPTER THIRTEEN

MR. PIERCE stepped out of his Ford. "At last," he exclaimed. "Where's Trooper and what about Jane?" Then he saw the Trumans and said, "Good evening."

"I'm afraid your girl's gone. The horse is on the other side of the bank," Mrs. Truman said.

"Gone?" said Mr. Pierce.

Angela explained and Mr. Pierce said testily, "Well, how am I to get at the horse if he's on the other side of the bank?"

The vet stepped forward then, and said, "I don't think we've met. I'm Saunders, from Betchley."

They talked for a time and then Mr. Pierce said, "Does anyone know where there's a gate?" He sounded crosser than ever.

After a time he drove away in the trailer and Mrs. Truman said, "Now he's here we may as well go home and see if Harriet's there yet."

"I suppose I'll have to go with him," Adam said.

"I think he should take Moonlight too," Professor Truman told them. "Angela's had enough for one day."

The vet climbed over the bank and started to pat Trooper and say, "Poor old fellow."

Adam thought, nearly home. Soon to-day will just seem like a bad dream.

"I'm all right," Angela said, but she didn't feel it, she felt exhausted, washed out like a damp rag hanging on a sagging line, she thought, looking at Trooper's bandaged leg and thinking, in spite of everything, Mr. Pierce isn't a bit pleased, and poor Jane's disappeared and may not be in hospital at all, and Harriet's lost. I really haven't been much good.

But the young vet seemed to read her thoughts, for he said, "I think you and the boy in the spectacles have been marvellous. Without you both, this horse would have lost gallons of blood, and if old Pierce isn't grateful he ought to be shot." He smiled at Angela and suddenly she felt better.

"I was just thinking that we'd been rather feeble," she said.

"I think you behaved very well indeed. I should hate to give up my shirt on a day like this," the vet said, trying to see Adam. "And you couldn't help it if the casualty walked."

Mr. Pierce arrived then with the trailer. And Professor Truman called from the other side, "I suppose you'll be giving Angela and her pony a lift home, Pierce."

Trooper was very lame and very stiff. He didn't want to move and it took all of them to get him into the trailer. After that Angela climbed over the bank, rode across the field to where there was a gate, and entered the field where the trailer was. The Trumans said, "We'd better be going," and started up their car and slid away into the darkness.

"I never have liked Mr. Pierce, but I like him even less to-day," Anne said.

"I wonder where Jane is. It's all rather horrible. I hope someone picks her up," said Mrs. Truman.

"Angela looked all in," remarked Professor Truman. They found the road quite easily.

"She's a nice girl, I can't see why you've always despised her, Anne," said Mrs. Truman.

"I haven't despised her, but she's always seemed so feeble. I can see now she isn't a bit," Anne replied.

"Are we on the right road, dear?" the professor asked.

"Yes, that's the park on your left," Mrs. Truman answered.

"I can see now that she's really rather nice," Anne continued. "It would be nice if we asked her over for a ride sometime, don't you think, Mummy?"

They crawled through Betchley; on the other side of the town the fog seemed still denser.

"I liked the young vet," Mrs. Truman said.

"We might ask Adam too," Anne mused. "He hasn't got a pony of his own."

"They ought to widen this road. It's a disgrace," observed Professor Truman.

"What's that in front?" asked Mrs. Truman. "It sounds like people talking."

"I can't hear a thing," replied Professor Truman.

"I can," shrieked Anne. "I can hear hoofs too."

*　　*　　*

"Thank goodness you're back at last, Guy," cried Mrs. Clavers as her husband came into the cottage. "Angela isn't back yet. What do you think's happened?"

"Good lord! But it's nearly seven. Doesn't anyone know where she is?" he asked.

Mrs. Clavers told him what she knew. When she had finished he said, "I suppose we'd better get the car out again and see whether we can find her. It's an awful night."

"I know, that's what makes it seem so much worse," his wife replied. "If she has hurt herself she might lie for hours in this fog."

They locked the back door and got out the car. "We'd better go along the Betchley road. They met in the town, didn't they?" Mr. Clavers asked.

*　　*　　*

Jane came to. She sat up with difficulty, because she was stiff; she thought, where am I? and remembered Trooper standing dejectedly by the bank. She thought, I must look for help, and started to walk. There was an aching feeling inside her. She wanted to cry, but no tears came.

She reached a road after stumbling across grass. She felt better with tarmac under her feet, but all the same she hardly cared whether she lived or died. She remembered Angela standing alone shivering in the fog and the dark and the damp air. She tried to hurry. She prayed, God help me to find help. Then she heard hoofs and it seemed that her prayer was answered. She thought, if only it's someone sensible, and wondered where Lucy and Graham were and what had happened to Adam.

Gradually the hoofs came nearer and she stood stock still in the middle of the road and her heart began to beat madly and she thought, don't let it be Mrs. Pierce. Oh God, let it be someone sensible. Then she heard a voice calling, "Hallo, is that Jane?" and she recognised it as Tony's, who she, like everyone else, thought of as "head in the air Selwyn Jones." She felt suddenly sick again and then she saw the dim outline of John and felt better.

"Thank God, we've found you," he said.

She wanted to cry on someone's shoulder. She wanted to be put to bed with a hot water-bottle and blankets which reached to her chin.

"We thought you were still by the bank. We sent an ambulance there," John said.

She could feel tears trickling down her face, though she hadn't realised she was crying.

"Ssh. She doesn't want to talk," Tony said, dismounting, taking Jane by the arm, saying, "You'd better sit down on my coat, while we think about help."

She said, "I don't want help. I'm quite all right." But it wasn't true, and she sat down gratefully on Tony's coat.

129

Gradually the hoofs came nearer

"She should have had mine," John said.

She sat bolt upright, because she didn't want to sleep again, and her arm ached, and she tried to move it and found she couldn't. She thought, it's broken and began to cry again.

"She's all in. You can see that. If only she had stayed by the bank," Tony said.

The hounds had started to lick the tears off Jane's face. Their tongues were soothing and she didn't push them away. She looked at Tony and thought, I don't believe she's conceited. She's nice; she's lent me her coat.

"We must do something," John said.

Then they all heard hoofs, small, brisk little hoofs which sounded cheerful on the tarmac.

"It sounds like ponies," John said.

"Hallo," shrieked Harriet into the dark. "Hallo. It's Lucy, Graham and Harriet. Who are you?"

"Damn," exclaimed John.

"They're better than no one," said Tony.

But why are they still out? They ought to have been home hours ago, thought Jane and felt a lump rising in her throat. I shall never be able to go back to the Lane End Riding School, she decided. They'll never forgive me for losing the children and hurting Trooper.

"John and Tony. We've found Jane," Tony shouted.

"Found Jane?" shouted Lucy and her voice was furious. "But we've sent an ambulance and a doctor and a vet, all to the bank in the vale." She thought, everything's ruined now. All that efficiency for nothing. "Why on earth did she move?"

"Don't be beastly," Tony said.

Harriet had dismounted. She hurried up to Jane and said, "How are you? Where's Angela? What happened?"

"Leave her alone. Or I'll brain all of you," John said.

"I decided to look for help because nothing came," Jane said.

"But we arranged everything beautifully. And now you've . . ." Lucy explained, but she never finished, because Harriet suddenly hit her violently across the shoulders with her hunting-whip.

"Shut up, you little beast," she screamed. "Leave Jane alone."

"Now they're off again. I wish I'd never come out to-day. I've missed a jolly good programme on TV, Ma's probably having kittens and I'm freezing," Graham complained.

Tony separated Harriet and Lucy.

"There's nothing we can do, is there?" Graham asked. "I really don't wish to waste any more time hanging about."

"Yes, we may as well go," Lucy said. "Jane isn't a bit grateful for all our efforts."

"I am. Thank you," said Jane.

"You needn't think I'm coming with you," Harriet cried.

"We don't want you, thank you," Lucy said.

"There's a car coming. I can see the lights," Tony said.

"We must stop it," said John, standing in the middle of the road and waving his arms.

But the car had already stopped. Out of it poured Anne and Jean, Professor and Mrs. Truman.

Anne gave a view holloa, which Harriet answered with an ear-splitting shriek, before she cried, "It's Mummy and Daddy and Anne and Jean. Oh, I'm so glad. Now everything will be all right."

Mrs. Truman said, "Good lord, it's Harriet."

"None the worse for her adventures by the sound of it," Professor Truman said.

"We've got Jane," Harriet shrieked.

"Not really. But how wonderful. How did she get here?" asked Mrs. Truman.

Everyone started to talk at once. Professor Truman

poured Jane a mug of coffee from the Thermos which wasn't yet empty.

"Let's see. Lots of sugar for shock, isn't it?" he asked his wife.

"That's right," she said.

"What's happened to Trooper?" Jane asked, sipping coffee.

Professor Truman sat beside her and explained about the trailer and the vet and Mr. Pierce. He purposely didn't mention the ambulances, but Jane kept asking about them, until finally he told her the truth. She said, "I've been a nuisance, haven't I?"

"Not at all. You've been a diversion for all of us. To-day we've lived," Professor Truman told her.

"We want you to come and stay when you've got time," Mrs. Truman said. "That is if you can bear the girls."

"Thank you very much," Jane said.

"Oh, how lovely," cried Harriet.

"If you've finished your coffee I think we'd better run you into hospital to have your arm X-rayed. Afterwards you can come back to the Mill House if you like," Mrs. Truman offered.

Jane wondered how she knew about her stiff arm. She thought, I should like to go to the Mill House. I like them all. They're friendly. She said. "Thank you very much," and thought, it's lovely to be organised.

"Harriet, you're to come in the car," Mrs. Truman told her. "Jean will ride Melody home."

Harriet's eyes filled with tears. "Can't I ride her home?" she wailed.

Jane had risen to her feet. She was hating the thought of hospital. She only wanted to climb into bed and sleep and sleep. Tony was looking at John, at his firm chin, his grey eyes and at the sticky mess which she knew was blood on his face. He's so good-looking. Mummy *must* like him, she thought. "Car, 'ware car," cried Anne.

John called hounds together. Everyone moved their horses and into their vision came a small red M.G. It stopped.

"What's this? A mother's meeting?" cried the voice of Mr. Jeeves.

"It's the Master," cried Harriet.

"Ssh," said Jean.

He stepped on to the road. "What's happened?" he asked. "Do you need any help?"

They could just see that he still wore his pink coat. He shook Professor and Mrs. Truman by the hand and said, "Hallo children," and when he saw John, "I want to see your father."

Jane remained obscured by the backs of the Trumans. She didn't want to see the Master. She felt guilty because she had caused so much trouble during the day.

Mrs. Truman started to relate the excitements of the evening, occasionally one of the others would chip in.

Jane sat down again with her head in her hands. It had been the longest day of her life and she wanted to forget it. Then she heard Mr. Jeeves say, "Is she here then?"

"Yes, but she ought to be in the casualty department of the hospital. We must get going," Mrs. Truman said.

"I've been wanting to see her ever since this morning. She sits marvellously. I want her to work in the Hunt Stables," he said.

Jane's head started to spin. It can't be true. I'm dreaming, she thought; but now he was coming towards her, and she raised her head and looked at his pink coat, and his gleaming buttons and then at his face. She thought, I'm not good enough. I should do something silly, I should fall off.

He looked at her and said, "Before you go into hospital will you promise me one thing—I don't know your name, but I've seen you ride."

134

She said, "What?" to gain time.

"Change your job. Come to the Hunt Stables when you come out?"

She thought, he thinks I'm going to be in hospital for a long time. Then she thought of working in the Hunt Stables, of all the horses she would ride, of hunting, of long lazy summers. She thought, I shan't have to answer advertisements, nor go back to the Pierces, and her spirits rose.

"If you think I'm suitable," she replied.

"That's settled then. But there's no need to come with a rush. Take a holiday first," he told her.

She thought, there'll be other grooms. I shall have a proper day off.

"I hope you'll ride second horse for me later on," Mr. Jeeves added.

"Hurray," cried Harriet. "You'll only be a few miles from us."

Mr. Jeeves, climbing into his M.G., felt satisfied. He had calmed Miss Mockler and engaged Jane. The Hunt Committee could take care of Freemantle. Now he only wanted his dinner, *Horse and Hound* and a cheerful fire. He called, "Look after yourselves," slipped in the clutch, shouted, "That's a promise. You can't take another job now," and slid away into the fog and dark.

"Gosh, Jane, you are lucky," cried Harriet.

"Come on, off to hospital," said Mrs. Truman, helping Jane into the Ford.

CHAPTER FOURTEEN

"IT'S NEARLY OVER," said Adam. "If only we knew where Jane was." He thought, to-morrow I shall wake up and all this will belong to the past. He took off his spectacles and wiped them.

"Yes, poor dear. I feel so awful about it all," Angela replied.

"Probably one of the ambulances has picked her up by now," exclaimed Mr. Pierce in heartless tones. He was sick of the day. His reputation had been ruined and though Trooper might recover he would be difficult to sell because of the accident. His wife's hunter was lame and they would be short-handed without Jane. He wanted to drive furiously hooting at all the corners, but he couldn't because of the fog and the trailer.

"She's so nice," Angela said.

Moonlight nuzzled Trooper. The fog seemed to be clearing. Nearly home, thought Adam.

*   *   *

"The fog's lifting, darling," said Guy Clavers driving into the road.

"I can't think why things always happen on a night like this," his wife said.

They both wore duffel coats. Mrs. Clavers had tied a scarf gypsy fashion round her head.

"Have a cigarette. They're in my pocket," Mr. Clavers said.

"I feel awful. Supposing she's really lost," his wife said.

*   *   *

Jane sat waiting in the casualty department of the Flintshire Hospital. Presently she was ushered into a small room where a young doctor in a white coat rose to greet her. In a kiosk along the passage Mrs. Truman was ringing up the Pierces.

"Let's have a look at you," the doctor said.

* * *

John and Tony rode home together. The fog had vanished as miraculously as it had come. A few moments back Jean had taken another road. Now they were alone together, with their horses, their tired hounds, with the silence of the night. For a time an uneasy silence fell between them. Then Tony said, "I've been wanting to talk to you for a long time, John." He couldn't see her face, but he turned his towards her. "I've been dying to with you too," he said.

"Isn't it silly that it takes an accident to break down the barriers we erect around ourselves," Tony told him.

"Or just an awful day, because it has been awful, hasn't it?" he asked.

"Yes, but lovely too," she replied, remembering their gallop together in the morning, their meeting together in the road and now the ride home.

He thought her voice sounded husky, and he said, "Anyway, it'll be all right now," and thought, I shall take her to dances, to the cinema and to point-to-points, if she'll come.

"I wish I was better at getting on with people," she told him.

"You are all right as you are," he said. Their horses walked side by side with loose reins. The sky cleared, until they could see a moon, proud and aloof in the dark sky.

Presently they came to the kennels, small and remote

in the moonlight. Hounds started to sing when they heard their hoofs. Tony looked at John and smiled.

*   *   *

Bill and Bruce arrived home. Their horses were tired; they themselves were weary and longed only for their suppers. Tom and Sam took their horses. "The Master's been back a long time," Sam told them.

"What about Captain Freemantle?" Bruce asked.

"Don't mention him," Bill said.

"He was back before two," Sam told them.

"The blighter," Bill exclaimed. "We're two and a half couple short, if he was any sort of a whip he would be out looking for them now."

They put hounds in kennel, looked them over for cuts and thorns, fed them.

"That's done them," Bill said, taking a Polo from the packet in his pocket. "Wish we hadn't lost the other two couple and a half though."

They turned to go to their houses; then they heard hoofs coming along the road.

"Better see who it is," Bill said.

*   *   *

Mark was nearly home. He seemed to have been trotting for hours. As he rode his mind went backwards and forwards over the day. He hoped the lost hounds would turn up, that John had recovered from his fall, that his mother wasn't anxious. At last the mist seemed to be clearing, and as he came to the village the moon appeared in the sky and he could see the Council cottages, very new and somehow prettier than usual in the moonlight.

*   *   *

Lucy and Graham came at last to the riding school.

"Gosh, I'm sore," complained Graham as they turned into the stableyard. "It's after eight," he added, looking at his watch. "By the time I'm home and had supper, I shall have missed all the things I wanted to see on TV."

"Do stop grumbling, no one would think you were a boy," replied Lucy.

Mrs. Pierce appeared from the saddle-room. She had changed into trousers and old gym shoes. She said, "I thought you were never coming. Your parents have been ringing up every five minutes."

"It wasn't our fault," exclaimed Graham, dismounting carefully.

"We were trying to help Jane. She met with an accident. I telephoned for everything, a vet, a doctor and an ambulance," Lucy told her.

"But it wasn't any good because she got up and walked and now . . ."

Lucy interrupted Graham. "Now she's gone into hospital with the Trumans," she said.

"Let's put the ponies away. Is she badly hurt?" inquired Mrs. Pierce.

"There's the telephone," Graham said. Mrs. Pierce vanished indoors.

"I wish she would ring up our parents, I want to go home," said Graham, who lived in a flat in the Rectory.

Mummy and Daddy will have had supper by now, the other children will be in bed, Lucy thought. I wish Jane hadn't left the bank, but I can still tell them about ordering everything, she decided.

She rubbed down Midnight and fetched him more water. Graham stood in the saddle-room and grumbled.

"Why don't you see to Jumbo?" Lucy asked.

"Why should I? I'm tired," Graham replied.

Presently Mrs. Pierce reappeared. "I've telephoned your parents. They won't be long," she said. "That was

Mrs. Truman. Jane's being looked after, so you've no need to worry any more."

"Here comes the trailer," cried Lucy, seeing lights coming along the road.

"It may only be a lorry," Graham said.

"At this time of night!" exclaimed Lucy.

They all hurried to meet Mr. Pierce. Adam and Angela climbed out of the car.

"I'm just going to drop Trooper, then I must take the kids and the grey pony home," Mr. Pierce said.

Trooper staggered painfully down the ramp into the yard. Angela felt a lump rising in her throat as she watched him.

Mrs. Pierce said, "He looks awful."

They put him in a box deeply bedded in straw. Moonlight whinnied.

"You can come home with me, Adam," Graham said.

"I'm going to ring you up, Adam. I want you to come and ride Moonlight some time," Angela told him.

"Thank you, thank you very much," he answered.

Angela clambered back into Mr. Pierce's car. "Don't be long," Mrs. Pierce called after them as they drove out of the yard into the moonlit night.

Graham's mother arrived. Tall and thin, with grey hair, she was still very angry. Adam, who hated rows, shrank away from her. He climbed into the back of her car and shut the door. But though he blocked his ears, he could still hear her voice going on and on at Mrs. Pierce. Finally she cried, "This is the last time Graham comes to your stables," and Mrs. Pierce said, "Just as you like," quite calmly, as though she didn't care. Then Graham and his mother joined Adam in the car.

"It's been a beastly day. I think hunting's wet," Graham said.

Adam sat in silence. He knew Graham considered him wet too, but he didn't care. He was to ride Moonlight.

The Trumans seemed to like him. Perhaps at last he was to have some real friends.

* * *

Lucy's father came. Big and friendly in a huge coat, he said, "Don't worry, Mrs. Pierce, these things will happen. Come along now, Lucy, your mother has supper and a hot bath waiting for you."

Lucy started to tell him about the accident as they walked out of the yard together to where his Hillman waited in the road.

"I telephoned lots of people," she cried in her rather high voice, "A doctor, a vet . . ."

* * *

Mrs. Truman had joined Jane and the doctor.

"I think we'll have to keep her to-night," he told Mrs. Truman. "Her arm's broken and she's suffering from concussion. If all goes well she might be able to go home to-morrow, but I'm afraid she'll have to spend the next few days in bed in a dark room."

Jane remained silent. Everything seemed out of her hands. She was happy to leave everything to Mrs. Truman.

"We'll ring up in the morning then. What about pyjamas and a tooth brush?" Mrs. Truman asked.

"We can provide something for to-night. She'll have to have an anaesthetic to have her arm set. I think she had better go into the casualty ward straight away," the doctor said.

It could be worse, Jane thought, a broken arm isn't much. . . . A nurse appeared with a wheel-chair.

"It's all right. I can walk," Jane said.

* * *

"There are lights on. They're still about," Tony said, riding into the kennel yard in a dream, thinking about John.

Bruce and Bill met them. "We've brought you some hounds," John said.

"I was wondering where they'd got to," Bill replied. "You haven't got old Thunder, by any chance?"

Tony thought, I must be sensible. He was an old hound after all. "He's dead," she said.

John started to explain. The yard was full of shadows. Hounds had stopped singing. Tony tried not to listen. She didn't want to remember Thunder lying dead on the road, to be filled with a useless remorse. Probably, as John said, it wasn't her fault. And anyway once she started thinking it was, she would go on for ever.

She thought of dinner in the dining-room at home. Of steaming soup, candlelight, of food and warmth; of telling her parents about the day, and taking off her boots.

"Oh, well, he was in his ninth season," Bill said. "I'm very grateful to you both for bringing the others home. Not that I'm not sorry about old Thunder."

"It's an awful shame," John said, hoping that Tony hadn't started to cry again.

"I'm sorry I couldn't stop the car," Tony said, turning round and looking at Bill.

"You did well to save the others. I might be two couples short, instead of one hound. I'm very grateful, miss," Bill said.

"Tony," she said, because he called John, John.

"We'd better go, I think. I'm sorry it was such a bad day. I expect you're tired," John remarked.

"Not too bad," Bill replied.

They rode away from the kennels and now they were nearly home. Soon we'll be each taking our separate roads, Tony thought.

Home, John thought. I hope they've kept some tea for me. He looked at his watch. "It's half past eight," he said.

They stood together

"Gosh, my parents must be in a flap," Tony exclaimed "Do yours flap?"

"Not much. Dad knows what hunting's like. He used to stag hunt in Devon and often he wouldn't be home till ten o'clock."

"How wonderful. Mummy does fuss rather. She imagines accidents."

"I should think we all will after to-day."

"How's your face?"

"Oh, all right. It isn't much."

They had both been waiting for the moment of parting. Now it had come. He said, "You won't forget about tea, will you?"

"Of course not. I'm looking forward to it. I hope your face won't keep you awake to-night."

They stood together and their horses nuzzled one another.

"I suppose we'd better be getting along," John said.

"Yes," she agreed. He touched her hand. "Well, goodbye," he said. "Look after yourself."

Tony shook his hand, because she wasn't sure what she was meant to do with it. Then she smiled, "I shall live for Wednesday," she said.

They took their separate roads with hopeful hearts. Tony thought, I do like him. He's the nicest person I've ever met.

Three days to Wednesday, thought John.

*   *   *

Angela was home. But only Solitaire, the Siamese cat, was in the kitchen to greet her. She gave Moonlight his mash with a sinking heart. Where were her parents? They must be looking for her. She searched for a message, but they had left none. She put on the kettle and made herself some tea.

CHAPTER FIFTEEN

MARK WAS home. Sitting in front of the kitchen stove he related the events of the day to his parents.

"It was a smashing day," he said. "And you should have seen old Merrylegs. The huntsman says she's as good as any of the big ones . . ."

In between talking he ate the rashers of bacon, the crisp fried bread and the eggs his mother had prepared for him. His sisters listened without much interest.

His father said, "She's a good pony. You couldn't have no better. Your mother was worried when it got so late."

"I thought you had an accident," his mother said. Mark pushed his dirty plate away and started to eat bread and butter and home-made jam.

"I've got a bit of pudding waiting for you in the oven," she said.

"Were there many out?" his father asked. Mark ate the pudding. He felt happy and pleasantly tired. In spite of the awful beginning, and the fog and the deer, it had been a lovely day, he felt; and he had been useful, and now he really knew the huntsman and the whip, he would be able to talk to them and learn the names of all the hounds and what the Pony Club Commissioner called the Science of Hunting.

"Not too many. About the usual," he told his father. "But I didn't really see them. I was helping the huntsman most of the time." He felt very grown up as he ate his pudding. He thought, I shall never forget to-day.

"I was afraid you were lost in the fog," his mother said.

"Merrylegs would have brought me back," Mark

replied, thinking, I must take her an apple before I go to bed.

"I've got the water hot so that you can have a bath," said his mother.

Mark told his parents more about his day, before he went along the road in the moonlight, and stood at the paddock gate calling, "Merrylegs, co'up Merrylegs."

*   *   *

The Trumans were home. They all had supper together in their long dining-room, which had a stone floor, yellow walls and a long modern table, which stood on trestles and could be taken to bits and used in the garden in the summer.

Harriet fell asleep almost as soon as she sat down. There were eggs and each of them had a different egg-cup, there were ham sandwiches cut by Ursula, mounds of bread and butter, an enormous fruit cake.

The children each had their own mug and drank milk. The cups and saucers were yellow like the walls.

It hadn't taken Jean long to ride Melody home and now the bay pony, like the other horses, was standing in the stable munching hay out of a net.

"Gosh, I never knew staying at home could be so exciting," Anne said, finishing her egg and taking a ham sandwich. "Don't you think Sandy was wonderful bringing Adam here?"

"He must have liked staying with us," Jean replied.

"Look at Harriet," Mrs. Truman said.

"I'm jolly glad Jane's coming to stay," exlaimed Anne. "I like her awfully."

"Where are her parents?" asked Jean.

"Dead," replied Mrs. Truman.

"Gosh, I was alseep!" exlaimed Harriet waking with a start.

"The sooner you're in bed the better," said Mrs. Truman.

"It was a lovely day. We really lived," said Harriet. She remembered the hours by the bank, her tears, riding away and afterwards the hours with Lucy.

"I don't like Lucy at all," she said.

Anne remembered the others leaving, her feeling f desolation, her lunch with Ursula, being lost, meeting Adam, her ride in the ambulance. It seemed a very long day. "It must be very late," she said.

Jean remembered being sorry for Anne as she rode out of the stableyard in the morning, she remembered falling off and her parents coming back with Black Knight; it had been awful wondering what had happened to Harriet, she remembered; but finally there had been the lovely ride home in the moonlight which had made up for everything. And now eating tea she was happy, because Jane was coming to stay and of all the people at the riding school she liked Jane best.

"We must remember to make up the spare room bed in the morning," said Mrs. Truman.

"It'll be nice to have Jane to stay," said Professor Truman. "Perhaps she'll improve your riding."

"Has she really got to stay in a dark room? How awful! I should go mad," Harriet said.

*   *   *

Tony rode into the stableyard. Mundy was waiting for her.

"I'm afraid I'm awfully late," she apologised. "All sorts of things happened."

"I thought you must be lost. That's what I thought," he said.

"I wish you hadn't waited for me. I could have put Southwind away," she replied, dismounting, discovering she was stiff, still thinking about John.

147

Mundy took Southwind. She went indoors, into the large hall, where her father's golf clubs stood in one corner and there was a silver salver on an oak chest.

Brutus ran to greet her. He put his paws on her shoulders and licked her face. Mrs. Selwyn Jones came out of the drawing-room. "Darling, we thought you were never coming back," she cried.

"It was the fog, and then there was an accident and a hound was run over," Tony said, taking off her bowler, running her hands through her hair, thinking, he must be home too by now.

"We waited dinner for you, so just wash your hands and come in. It doesn't matter about your boots," her mother said.

She washed her hands in the downstairs cloakroom. There was soup, followed by a joint and vegetables, followed by vanilla ice-cream and biscuits and cheese.

Tony told her parents about the day as she ate. Somehow none of it seemed quite real any more. And all the time she was remembering, *Splashing along the boggy rides all day* . . . the whole poem was running through her head as she ate and talked.

After dinner she sat for a time in the drawing-room and told her parents about John, and that she hoped he would come to tea some time. She hadn't meant to mention him, but suddenly she felt she must tell someone. There was an open fire blazing, big armchairs, Brutus lay at her feet. The morning, the run, the death of Thunder, even the ride home all seemed to belong to another day.

"You must be very tired," her mother said.

"I thought you would come home as soon as the fog appeared, I didn't think hounds hunted in a fog," her father told her.

"They don't usually," she replied, wondering whether John had washed the blood off his face yet. "It was because they got mixed up with the deer, otherwise we'd have

148

packed up by three at the latest." But she was glad they hadn't. Because except for poor Thunder and Jane, the day had been marvellous, she decided, watching the firelight playing on the walls, Brutus twitching in his sleep. She wanted to stay up for hours thinking, but quite suddenly she fell asleep.

*　　*　　*

Mr. Jeeves drove into the kennel yard. He looked at hounds slumbering now on their benches. Then he sauntered down to Bill's cottage.

He knocked on the door and then walked in. Bill was sitting by an open range. His wife was making tea.

"I did knock," said Mr. Jeeves. Over the chimney piece hung a picture of Queen Victoria and Prince Albert. It had belonged to Bill's mother. On the floor were the skins of dead hounds used now as rugs.

Bill stood up. " 'Evening, sir," he said.

"Are they all on?" asked Mr. Jeeves. Bill told him about Thunder's fate and about Tony and John bringing two couples home. Mrs. Smart poured them all cups of tea.

"I'm glad about the others, sickening about Thunder though, good thing he was an old hound," said Mr. Jeeves.

"It will happen. The blighters won't stop," said Bill, alluding to the drivers of motor cars.

Presently Mr. Jeeves said, "Captain Freemantle will have to go. I've been on to the Hunt Committee to-night about it. He's no use at all."

It seemed to Bill then that a great weight was lifted from his mind. When Mr. Jeeves had come into the cottage he had thought he had come to give him notice. Now he knew he was to stay.

"He never has been much good," he said.

"And I'm employing that fair girl who's been working

149

at Pierces'. I want her to ride second horse. Sam's getting past it," Mr. Jeeves continued.

A little later he left. And Bill turned to his wife and said, "He's all right, isn't he? Some difference between him and Captain Freemantle."

He thought, Sam'll be glad to stop riding second horse. I wonder who'll whip-in now with Bruce?

*   *   *

At the Four Feathers, Tom was playing darts.

"A double six and you'll be out, Tom," a young mechanic from the garage said.

Tom took careful aim, threw his dart.

"He's done it," someone cried.

He walked forward and pulled his dart from the double six.

*   *   *

Peter, John's youngest brother, met him in the yard. "We thought you were never coming. Mum's been scared."

His father opened the back door. "Is that you, John?" he called.

"Yes, sorry to be so late," John called back. The cows were milked, the farmyard deserted.

His father came out of the house with a bucket. "I've got a warm feed for her," he said.

Together they took off Quickstep's tack, rubbed her down and put on her rugs. "What sort of day did you have?" asked Mr. Simons.

They walked into the house together talking. Half of John was still with Tony, it had been like that the whole of the last bit home.

The teapot was waiting on the stove. But Mrs. Simons

insisted on making another pot. There was a leg of ham on the table, a piece of cheese, pickles, biscuits, cake.

"I've kept a bit of lunch for you. I thought you'd like something hot," his mother said. He was too tired to take off his boots. He sat down as he was and ate and then his mother saw the blood on his face and cried "John, what have you done?"

He said, "It's nothing," but it wasn't any use. He had to go upstairs to the bathroom and have it washed and bathed in antiseptic, and when he looked in the mirror he saw that he had a black eye and the whole of the left side of his face was swollen.

"You've made a proper mess of yourself," his mother said.

He went back to the kitchen and finished his meal. He told his parents about the day and lived it again as he talked. He remembered how he had quarrelled with Tony on the plough, the gallop afterwards through the park, being dragged off, finding Tony in the road, the ride home. If it hadn't been for the fog it might have been quite an ordinary day, he thought; as it is it's a day I shall never forget. He didn't say, to-day I lived, like Harriet, but he felt that he had grown up suddenly. He felt altogether different and much more competent. It must be because of Tony, he thought.

He poured himself another cup of tea, though he had drunk three already.

"I've invited Tony Selwyn Jones to tea," he said.

*   *   *

Jane was propped up with pillows eating supper. There were eleven other casualties in the ward and most of them were old ladies who had slipped and broken their legs.

Her arm was set and, in spite of the anaesthetic, she was feeling better. She thought, to-morrow I shall go to

151

the Trumans, and after that to my new job at the Hunt stables. Suddenly her future seemed marvellously secure. She thought, I never imagined my life could change so much in a day, and then, I do hope Trooper's going to be all right.

The old lady in the next bed said, "How do you feel, dear? Better?"

"Yes, thank you. Have you got a broken leg?" she asked.

"Thigh, dear. I've been in here nine weeks," the old lady said.

A young nurse brought the pudding. She looked at Jane and said. "Don't talk too much," and gave her a helping of trifle.

Hunting, taking Midnight to the forge in the morning, the ride to the meet, talking to John and Tony seemed to have taken place years ago. As for the hunt, Jane couldn't remember any of it. She finished her trifle and lay down again.

"Nice, wasn't it?" the old lady asked.

*　　*　　*

Bruce lodged with Sam and his wife. They all sat talking now, round the ancient range in Sam's small homely kitchen.

They had washed down their supper with beer.

"Have you heard Freemantle's going?" Bruce asked.

"About time too," Sam said.

"And there's a girl coming to ride second horse," Bruce continued.

"A girl?" exclaimed Sam.

"That's right," said Bruce.

"Well, I never," said Sam's wife.

*　　*　　*

152

Adam thanked Graham's mother. Then he ran ahead across the Rectory drive, opened the front door and cried, "Mummy, I'm home."

His father was preparing a sermon in the study, which he used for work and for seeing parishioners.

His mother came out of the kitchen with an apron on. "I'm so glad you're home," she cried and kissed Adam.

He could hear Graham and his mother going up to the flat above. In the other flat the wireless was on. As usual, the Rectory was cold. Adam shivered.

"Come in by the fire and have your supper and tell me all about the day. Whatever happened?" his mother asked.

His father peered round the study door. "Everything all right?" he asked.

There was hot soup, scrambled eggs on toast, fruit salad.

"The fog was awful," Adam said. "There was an accident . . ."

When he had finished telling his story, his mother said, "Poor Adam. What an awful day. Where's the girl now?"

"In hospital. She's going to stay with the Trumans when she comes out. And do you know, Angela Clavers has invited me to ride Moonlight. She's going to ring me up."

It wasn't often Adam received an invitation and he knew his mother would be pleased.

"Oh, how nice. Oh, I am glad," she said.

"And the Trumans were awfully friendly and I like Anne very much. Can we ask them to tea some time, please?" In spite of the awfulness of the day, now sitting by the fire Adam had no sense of failure, rather the reverse in fact. "In lots of ways it's been a lovely day," he said, forgetting the awful hours when he was lost, the humiliating time when he couldn't direct the ambulance to the bank, the ghastly moment of arrival only to discover Jane had vanished.

"Can I hunt next week? Or is it too expensive?" he asked.

* * *

While his mother got supper, Graham switched on the television. He had told his mother all about the day as they had driven home together. Now he only wanted to relax in a chair and watch the Variety Show which was on TV. He ached all over and he was sore. His mother had told him to have a hot bath, but he had pretended not to hear. He thought, "Never again. How people can go hunting week after week I can't imagine."

Then he began to laugh as a comedian appeared and started to crack jokes.

* * *

Lucy ate her supper off a tray in front of the nursery fire.

"It was a most exciting day," she said for the third time. "I do want to hunt again."

"I don't want you to have an accident," her mother said.

"I shan't Gosh, Graham was feeble. I never want to hunt with him again," Lucy said. "Next time I shall follow the Master."

"You must be careful," said her mother.

"I will be," Lucy promised, wishing that the rest of the family were still up so that she could tell them about her day.

* * *

The Pierces didn't talk much as they ate their supper.

Once Mr. Pierce said, "I think Trooper will get over it, but it'll take time and will most likely leave a scar."

"We'd better start looking for a new girl, it will be weeks before Jane can come back," Mrs. Pierce said.

"I'll draft out an advertisement for *Horse and Hound*. It's a nuisance because she was a good worker," Mr. Pierce replied.

"The bank was much too high and difficult for the horse. She shouldn't have attempted it," said Mrs. Pierce.

"Pass the bread, please," said Mr. Pierce.

*   *   *

Captain Freemantle was telling his guests about his day. "They ran marvellously in the morning. But later they lost and then the fog came down, so I called it a day," he said.

"Is it a good pack?" someone asked.

"Small, but sporting. I whip-in, you know," replied Captain Freemantle.

*   *   *

At nine o'clock Mr. and Mrs. Clavers returned to their cottage. Angela was waiting for them by the garden gate.

"Thank goodness. At last!" she cried. "I've been back ages."

She kissed Moonlight good night, before she went indoors with her parents. The night was bright and full of a million stars. I must ring up to-morrow and find out how Jane is, she thought, turning away from the loose-box to the cottage so romantic beneath the moon.

She told her parents about the day while her mother cooked bacon and eggs on the Aga. "I'm sorry you had to look for me," she apologised. "I meant to ring up

155

She kissed Moonlight good night

from the riding school but the Pierces seemed awfully cross and I didn't like to ask."

"We try not to be fussing parents, but when one's daughter isn't home from hunting by eight o'clock one's bound to worry," her father said.

"Mrs. Pierce said you were with Jane, but somehow it didn't help," Mrs. Clavers told her.

"I'm awfully sorry," Angela said again, and then, "Can I have Adam Clarke to tea some time please?"

"You mean the Rector's son?" her father asked.

"That's right!" said Angela.

* * *

Mr. Jeeves was reading *Horse and Hound*. "Time we had a twelve mile point and sent in a report," he told his wife. "Still, I think Bill Smart's a good man with hounds. When we've got rid of Freemantle things should be better."

* * *

In the kennels the tired hounds slept. The moon rode high over Flintshire, beneath it the vale was full of the glamour of night. In the park the deer grazed peacefully. In Betchley the market-place was deserted. There was nothing now to remind anyone of the disastrous hunt across the vale.

THE END

CHRISTINE PULLEIN-THOMPSON

Five thrilling books by Christine Pullein-Thompson about Phantom, the beautiful, wild Palomino whom no one could capture.

PHANTOM HORSE

The story of how Angus and Jean go to America, and catch their first glimpse of Phantom in the Blue Ridge Mountains. They are determined to catch him – but so are others, whose motives are sinister . . .

PHANTOM HORSE COMES HOME

Phantom is Jean's greatest joy, but wildness is still in his blood – and when the family has to move back to England, Jean knows he'll never stand the plane journey. Halfway across the Atlantic, Phantom goes mad . . .

PHANTOM HORSE GOES TO IRELAND

A trip to Killarney with Phantom and Angus will be a wonderful holiday, Jean imagines. But it is not the peaceful place she expects. Strange noises are heard in their host's house at night – and then Angus is kidnapped . . .

PHANTOM HORSE IN DANGER

Angus and Jean devise a daring plan to rescue Angus's horse, Killarney, from a cruel horse dealer. But the plan goes horribly wrong. Terror-struck, they realise they may never see Phantom alive again . . .

PHANTOM HORSE GOES TO SCOTLAND

An idyllic Scottish island becomes a terrifying prison for Angus and Jean when they witness the kidnapping of a team of Olympic show-jumpers. Trapped by the criminals, Jean and Phantom are forced to make a dare-devil swim through rough seas in a bid to save Angus's life.

Armada

'JINNY AT FINMORY' BOOKS
by Patricia Leitch
Armada Originals

FOR LOVE OF A HORSE
Red-haired Jinny Manders has always dreamt of owning a horse. When she rescues Shantih, a chestnut Arab mare, from a cruel circus, her wish seems about to come true. But Shantih escapes on to the moors above their home where Jinny despairs of ever getting near her again.

A DEVIL TO RIDE
Shantih, safe for the first time in her life, in the Manders' stable, is inseparable from her new mistress. But she is impossible to ride, and Jinny can't control her . . .

THE SUMMER RIDERS
Jinny is furious when Marlene, the brash city girl, comes to stay and insists on riding Shantih. But when Marlene's brother, Bill, gets into trouble with the local police, Jinny and Shantih are the only ones who can stop him being prosecuted.

NIGHT OF THE RED HORSE
When archaeologists come to Finmory to excavate an ancient site, Jinny and Shantih mysteriously and terrifyingly fall under the power of ancient Celtic 'Pony Folk'.

GALLOP TO THE HILLS
Jinny's special friend, Ken, leaves Finmory and his dog, Kelly, disappears. Sheep are killed on the moor and local farmers set out to hunt Kelly down – and Jinny and Shantih find themselves involved in a desperate race to save him.

HORSE IN A MILLION
Life seems to fall apart for Jinny when Shantih disappears from her field one night. Desperate to find her, Jinny begins a desperate race against time – a race that takes her away from the wild Finmory hills and into danger.

Armada

CAPTAIN ARMADA

has a whole shipload of exciting books for you

Here are just some of the best-selling titles that Armada has to offer:

☒ **Phantom Horse Goes to Scotland** Christine Pullein-Thompson 80p

☒ **Improve Your Riding** Christine Pullein-Thompson 65p

☒ **Jump to the Top** Patricia Leitch 80p

☒ **Horse in a Million** Patricia Leitch 75p

☒ **Show Jumping Secret** Josephine Pullein-Thompson 80p

☒ **Pony Club Team** Josephine Pullein-Thompson 75p

☒ **Three Ponies and Shannan** Diana Pullein-Thompson 80p

☒ **Ponies in the Valley** Diana Pullein-Thompson 75p

☒ **Black Beauty** Anna Sewell 65p

☒ **Jackie and the Phantom Ponies** Judith M. Berrisford 80p

Armadas are available in bookshops and newsagents, but can also be ordered by post.

HOW TO ORDER

ARMADA BOOKS, Cash Sales Dept., GPO Box 29, Douglas, Isle of Man, British Isles. Please send purchase price of book plus postage, as follows:—

    1—4 Books .... 10p per copy

    5 Books or more .... no further charge

    25 Books sent post free within U.K.

Overseas Customers: 12p per copy

NAME (Block letters)

_____

ADDRESS

_____

_____

_____